PRAISE FOR THE DIANA HUNTER SERIES

"Awesome."

"On the edge of my seat..."

"Page turner."

"I cannot tell you the last time a group of characters endeared me as quickly..."

"Diana Hunter is a strong, intelligent, and very likeable heroine."

"Grabbed me from the first page, and I sat up until 4:30 in the morning reading it."

"The story line is quick-paced and attention-holding. This one deserves 5+ stars."

"This book will keep you turning the pages to find out the who, what, why, and how."

"Couldn't put it down!"

"Left me wanting more."

"Peter and Diana have a great chemistry."

"I love the author's writing."

"A pleasure to read."

"Really captivating."

"Fast-paced, well-written, fun stories."

EXPOSED

BOOKS IN THE DIANA HUNTER SERIES

Hunted (Prequel)

Snatched

Stolen

Chopped

Exposed

Broken

COLLECTIONS

Books 1-3

Snatched

Stolen

Chopped

Published by Mesa Verde Publishing
P.O. Box 1002
San Carlos, CA 94070

ISBN: 978-1545147337

"A great book should leave you with many experiences and slightly exhausted at the end. You live several lives while reading."

- William Styron -

EXPOSED

A. J. GOLDEN

GABRIELLA ZINNAS

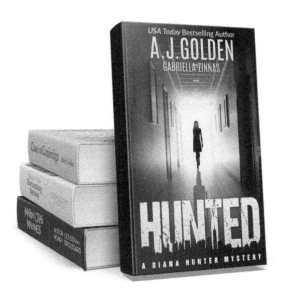

"Your emails seem to come on days when I need to read them because they are so upbeat."
- Linda W -

For a limited time, you can get the first books in each of my series - *Chaos in Cambridge, Hunted* (exclusively for subscribers - not available anywhere else), *The Case of the Screaming Beauty,* and *Mardi Gras Madness* - plus updates about new releases, promotions, and other Insider exclusives, by signing up for my mailing list at:

https://www.alisongolden.com/diana

PROLOGUE

SALAH SAT SILENTLY in the back seat. Abdel and Jawad were talking urgently in the front. Hip-hop was coming out of the speaker by Salah's head, the staccato beat of the words at odds with the bass note of the track. Salah leaned over.

"Here."

"What, bro?" Abdel was driving. He glanced into his rearview mirror to look at the boy in the back seat. Black fuzz peppered Salah's upper lip and his chin.

"Drop me here. I'll walk the rest of the way," Salah said softly.

"You sure?" Abdel pulled the car over.

"Yeah, I'm sure."

With a languid stretch, Salah opened the door and loped out, dragging his backpack behind him. He hefted it onto his shoulder in one smooth move.

Jawad wound down the passenger door window. "See you in a few, okay?"

"Yeah, see ya."

The black BMW flicked its lights on and pulled away.

Salah, his head down as he took the pack's weight, turned toward home. He walked past the shops and businesses that lined the main road: a loan shark, a barber shop, and an auto repair. They were all closed now. A takeout advertised "Authentic Salvadorian Food." Often, Salah would stop to pick up something, but today he didn't feel hungry. Instead, he kept on, his tall, sloping gait telegraphing his mood better than any words.

It started to drizzle. Salah thought back to the events of his day. Things had begun as a bit of a laugh, then morphed into a mixture of excitement and danger, a personal calling, and finally, a noble cause. Now though, he wasn't so sure.

Salah walked up the path to his family home. He put the key in the lock, opening the front door of the wooden-slatted bungalow. It was badly in need of repair, almost a shack. The black door was smeared with white paint. Someone had attempted to clean off graffiti and given up halfway through. Rusted, broken guttering hung uselessly from a gable. Two of three front windows were boarded up.

Salah's family's detritus littered the front yard—mostly sodden cardboard and plastic cartons. No one had cleared it in months, his mother too busy working her three jobs, his father struggling to manage the cancer the doctors had taken too long to diagnose. Salah and his brothers didn't care for yard work.

Salah shut the front door with a bang and walked to the bedroom he shared with his two siblings. It was empty. He flung his backpack onto his bed and sat down heavily. With his elbows on his knees, he put his head in his hands, his fingers splaying around his eyes as he stared at the faded, filthy carpet. He sat immobile, deep in thought before he heard his father's voice, weak and tremulous, calling his name. Salah stood wearily. "Coming!"

The tall, skinny-framed boy propped himself against the wall of the bedroom. His brown eyes, framed with lashes so long that girls at school teased him, blinked as he looked out the window. White emulsion, inexpertly applied, was now cracking and peeling away from the metal window frame.

Salah, who'd loved the escape from daily life that English Literature provided when he was in school, ruefully considered the metaphor. The cracked, peeling paint revealed the hard, joyless frame just as the forced curtailing of Salah's education exposed his lost self. He missed the rhythm of language, how it moved him, and introduced him to new worlds and ways of thinking. Salah missed his friends, his teachers, and their collaboration.

Hearing his name again, Salah returned to the present. He looked out at the dreary view from his window a moment longer before he pushed himself off the wall and went to his father. Mostly, he missed the feeling of hope.

DIANA REACHED FOR the hem of her jacket with both hands and smartly pulled it down as she looked at herself in the mirror with a critical eye. It had been a while since she had worn her military greens. It was almost like looking at someone else in the mirror. Her demeanor changed. She stood stiffly, shoulders back, chin up. Military posture.

For Diana, the uniform represented more than just a different set of clothing. She considered wearing it a responsibility, one she never took lightly, and a privilege. Inspecting herself, making sure everything was in place and properly presented, acted to infuse into her being the essence of a culture and code in which every man and woman would lay down their life for her, who would have her back, as she would theirs.

Diana had donned her combat fatigues. She would be flying to an American base near Seattle and boarding a military transport plane headed out to Kandahar, called there at the request of Major Ethan Lennox, head of Task Force Indigo. She wouldn't need her dress uniform in

Afghanistan, that's for sure. Diana gave herself another once over, patting her regulation bun to make sure it was fastened securely. She left her bedroom and walked down the hall to the guest room, the door of which she always kept closed.

The room was the same as always. Of course, it was. Diana was the only person allowed in there. Pictures and photographs spread all around the white walls of the room. A whiteboard with scribbled notes interrupted the family scenes. A white sofa faced it.

Diana sat on the sofa and shut her eyes. This was another ritual she always followed before a major op. It had been over ten years now since they died, but she could still hear her parents' voices and conjure up their faces if she concentrated hard enough. Sometimes they came unbidden into her consciousness and caught her unawares, but only if she dropped her emotional defenses. Diana was well-practiced in maintaining them and they fell only rarely. She had a purpose and things she had to do. Dwelling too much on her life "before" would not help her. Instead, everything and everyone was measured and monitored so they didn't overwhelm her and render her lost in a sea of dysfunctional feelings.

With a deep breath, Diana opened her eyes and pushed herself out of the sofa. As she left the room, she set the catch to lock. It wouldn't do for anyone to see inside while she was gone.

"You look different, somehow," Terri said as she came out of the kitchen, a sandwich in hand. Terri was Diana's dog walker who'd come to look after Diana's dog, Max, while Diana was away.

A few days prior, Terri had been captured and held hostage by an assassin who had used the young woman to bait Diana. After the dramatic rescue that involved a snarling Max and a plethora of big men with guns, Diana never expected to see her dog sitter again. But to her surprise, the student had been more than happy to stay with Max for the duration of Diana's trip.

"Well, I am wearing a uniform," Diana said.

Terri shook her head. "It's not that. Yeah, I haven't seen you in your army gear before, but you're different somehow."

"Is it that I have a don't-mess-with-her air about me?" Diana raised her eyebrows. "Is that what you're saying?"

"Oh no, that's your normal look," Terri grinned. "I mean there's something more about you. Steely."

"I look steely, huh? And I don't normally? I'm not sure Peter would agree with you." Peter Hopkinson was Diana's partner. He was going to Afghanistan with her.

"Oh, I don't know. You don't always play hardball with him." Terri flicked up her eyebrows and smiled conspiratorially as she took a big bite of her sandwich. Diana squinted, not sure of Terri's meaning, before adjusting her cuffs and patting down her jacket.

"Well, that's good. Steely. Hardball. That's the look I'm aiming for," Diana said, standing up straight.

Terri giggled. "Well, you've succeeded." She paused for a moment to take another bite while Diana checked to make sure she had taken care of everything for her trip. She may look like a woman of steel, but she still had to take care of paying the bills, leave money for dog food, and other mundane day-to-day things. Being a hotshot wasn't all that, all the time.

"So, when do you leave?" Terri asked, interrupting Diana's train of thought.

Diana glanced at the time. "They should be here any—"

Before she could finish her sentence, her phone rang. "And they're here." It was Peter.

"I'll be right out," she said into the phone. A car had been sent to take them to Canadian Forces Base Comox. Diana grabbed her regulation gym bag and kissed Terri on the cheek. "Take care, hun."

Diana dropped to her haunches and gave Max a good scratch. The little Maltese terrier wagged his tail but looked so forlorn that Diana steeled herself for real. He knew she'd be away for a while. He'd seen her packing. "You're too smart for your own good," Diana said. "I'm going to miss you, boy."

At that, Max let out a plaintive whine that nearly brought tears to Diana's eyes. He was used to her going off for a few weeks every once in a while, and this time she didn't expect to be gone nearly that long, but her small fluffy dog had emotional manipulation down pat. Max was more skilled in breeching Diana's emotional defenses than any human, but she knew from experience that as soon as she walked out the door, he'd be more than happy with Terri. Until she left, however, he would do his best to blackmail her into not going.

"Mommy loves you, baby," she said. "I'll be back soon."

"Go on, we'll be fine," Terri promised.

Diana smiled at her. "I know you will. So, you've got everything you need, right?"

"Absolutely. Stop worrying, everything will be fine. And yes, I know, if I'm even slightly suspicious or worried, I can call any of the numbers you gave me, and the cops will be at the door in minutes."

Diana nodded. She'd spoken to Donaldson, the superintendent of VPD Major Crimes Division and her superior. The Surgeon, the professional hitman who had taken Terri hostage, had been shipped off to a maximum security jail from which he would be transferred to Guantánamo Bay but Diana still felt uncomfortable leaving Terri alone in her apartment with Max. Bill Donaldson had promised to check in on Terri regularly. He also gave her his personal cell-phone number. Terri could call him if anything concerned her, and he'd send the troops in.

"Okay, I'm off. If anything, anything at all happens, even if you think it's just your imagination, you make the call," Diana insisted.

Loose ends dangled over Diana. Before holding her dog sitter hostage, The Surgeon had been hired by a Canadian security firm to kill another assassin, a rival whose target had been Riley Greene, a Canadian senator. The motive for the hit on Greene was unresolved and bothering Diana. The story had not yet run its course, and finding out more was the reason for the trip to Kandahar. Diana wondered what she and Peter would discover.

Back in her apartment, Terri put her hand over her heart. "I swear, I will call the superintendent if so much as a mouse spooks me," she said with a grin. Then Terri sobered. "Don't worry, Diana. I promise Max will be safe."

Diana sighed and dropped her bag onto the floor. "I want you *both* safe," she said as she pulled the girl into a hug. She'd grown quite fond of Terri despite her best efforts. Terri had a lovely personality. She was bubbly and cheerful, and she adored Max. While they didn't exactly share makeup and clothes, Diana had warmed to her. It was almost like having a little sister.

Terri hugged Diana back just as hard. "I promise, we'll be fine," she said. "Now, you go and kick some terrorist butt so that we can all be safe." Diana's eyes widened just a smidgeon. "Or whatever it is you're doing," Terri added quickly.

"Okay, I'm off," Diana said with a smile. She picked up her bag, turned around, and walked out of her apartment, closing the door behind her. She refused to look back because she knew Max would get to her again. A captain in the Canadian Military Intelligence Branch, or INT for short, could not show signs of weakness. She had to be in control at all times.

CHAPTER TWO

I N THE ELEVATOR, Diana again checked herself in the mirror. She nodded at her reflection, satisfied. There was no trace of any emotional display. When the doors opened, she walked out into the low-lit, neutral-toned lobby of her apartment building.

"Ma'am?" Jimmy, the daytime doorman, greeted her as he popped up from behind the counter. On it, that week's large floral arrangement of lilies, gladioli, and heavenly-scented jasmine was in full bloom.

"Hello, Jimmy."

Jimmy's eyes widened. "Ms. Hunter? I didn't even recognize you!" he exclaimed.

"It's okay, Jimmy. I'm off for a few days. Remember, Terri's staying at my place. Would you mention that to Larry? I did tell him, but it would help if you'd remind him." Larry was the nighttime doorman and Jimmy's brother.

Jimmy nodded quickly. "Sure, and I'll check in on Ms. Jenkins every once in a while. I'll make sure she's okay, and that no more unpleasantness occurs."

"Thanks, Jimmy."

"Have a safe trip, Ms. Hunter."

Diana smiled and walked out onto the sidewalk. A big, black SUV was waiting out front like a big inkblot in the early morning sunshine. Peter leaned against it, his arms folded, talking to two men in uniform. He looked good in his combat gear.

Diana glanced at the two men that Peter was talking to. They stood sideways to her, their features obscured. She also couldn't see their rank. That didn't mean Diana couldn't make a few deductions, though.

Their situation didn't call for any military stance, but one of the men stood "at ease." He was likely subordinate. He also didn't speak unless directly addressed, though he did make eye contact. Every time he glanced at his superiors, his micro-expressions revealed respect and deference. Micro-expressions last for less than a fifth of a second and are unconscious, devoid of manipulation, and completely genuine. Noticing and interpreting them was Diana's specialty.

The other man's stance was more casual, but he was a little stiffer. This man was more animated than the other who was at ease, but his micro-expressions transmitted respect and admiration for Peter, his eyes flickering intermittently as the two men chatted.

As she drew near, Diana cleared her throat. The military strangers turned to her, snapped to attention, and saluted. "Captain!"

Diana had been right about their ranks. One was a lieutenant, the other a corporal. Peter didn't move.

"At ease, Lieutenant, Corporal . . . ?" Diana trailed off.

"Lieutenant Toby Mizota, ma'am," the taller of the two men responded quickly. His stance relaxed.

"Corporal Rodney Jones, ma'am," said the other, still standing stiffly to attention.

"Well, good morning, Lieutenant Mizota and Corporal Jones. Let's get this show on the road, shall we?" Diana ignored Peter.

The corporal grabbed Diana's bag and moved to open the back passenger doors. As Diana and Peter climbed into the back seats, the corporal slung Diana's bag into the trunk and they were off.

Peter leaned toward Diana. "Good morning, *Captain*," he murmured.

"It's not quite as impressive as it sounds," Diana whispered staring straight head. "But it is classified." Now it was her turn to lean in. "*Major*."

Peter leaned away and looked out the window, a slight smile playing across his lips. Almost no one at VPD knew what he'd done previously. He'd kept it to himself. He liked it better that way. It prevented people from asking awkward questions, like why a former army major was now a lowly detective in the local police department.

"That's two stories you owe me," Peter replied. "I guess it won't be such a boring flight, after all." Still looking out the window, he grinned.

Diana smiled at him ruefully. She had worked for TFI on and off for a while now but hadn't told Peter until recently. He'd been upset with her for holding back. Her insistence that he accompany her to Kandahar was a form of apology, and she realized with a jolt she was increasingly dependent upon him. They worked well together, and she liked having him by her side.

Once ordered to Kandahar, Peter was back on active duty within hours. Task Force Indigo held a lot of sway. It was the first and best line of defense against terrorism worldwide. There was good reason there had been no major coordinated attacks in the UK, Canada, and the US for over ten years now and the existence of TFI was a large part of it.

TFI operated all over the world, wherever a terrorist threat arose. They had been operating mainly in the Middle East for a while, but they had people on the ground in South America and Africa too. Domestic branches in each of the member countries existed to gather intelligence and oversee security threats. Over its ten-year history, TFI had prevented dozens of terror attacks, often in the planning stages, saving tens of thousands of lives. Rarely did the public hear of their work.

Peter had a stellar record, and his special forces experience had made it straightforward to get his security clearances reinstated. Diana had made some calls to speed up the process and learned the highlights of Peter's military career. It had been most impressive. Peter had led his team on many dangerous missions and distinguished himself as a strong, fearless, and respected leader. His unit had become the go-to team for the missions that others wouldn't or couldn't pull off; the ones marked chaos, high risk, and violent.

Plus, Peter always made sure to stay out of the spotlight. Along with his range of skills, including intelligence gathering, he would have made a perfect addition to TFI. Diana wondered if he had been offered a position. With TFI, there was no glory, no recognition, nothing, just a quiet satisfaction, and a passion for the work and its outcome. That would have suited Peter perfectly. Diana glanced around her and realized, much to her surprise, that they'd already arrived at Horseshoe Bay Ferry Terminal. She must have been lost in her thoughts for far longer than she'd realized.

"How are you doing?" Peter asked suddenly, startling her, though he kept his voice low.

Diana whipped her head around to stare at him. "What do you mean?" she asked softly.

"The other night wasn't what I'd call a fun evening at home," he said with a small shrug. His eyes were filled with concern for her. "Terri, okay?"

"Yes, seems to be. Max slept most of yesterday, but he was back on form this morning. Tried to emotionally blackmail me when I left."

Peter snickered. Diana's heart softened, and she smiled gently at him. She inched her hand across the space that separated them, trying her best to make sure the two men up front didn't notice. She curled her hand into Peter's and squeezed. "I'm good," she said. "Been through worse."

"But still, sure you're okay?"

"Perfect. Let's hope The Surgeon doesn't get out again, eh?"

"I highly doubt he will. He's in solitary. I promise he was well and truly locked up and subject to three levels of security when I left. It would take an army to spring him from there," Peter murmured. Thirty-six hours ago, Diana ordered that Peter escort The Surgeon to jail. She didn't trust anyone else with the job.

"Thank you for making sure. I feel better knowing that you were there," Diana said.

"My pleasure," Peter responded. "I'll always have your back," he said softly. He squeezed her hand gently. She smiled at him, but just as she was about to say something more, a movement in front drew her attention. The lieutenant had shifted, trying to get a better view of them in the wing mirror. He probably thought they had no clue he was spying on them, but Diana noticed the minutest of signs. To her, a tiny shift to the side was like someone waving a red flag. She glanced at Peter and inclined her head toward the lieutenant. Peter looked over at Mizota. He let go of her hand.

"I'm going to get some sleep," he said.

"Me too," Diana replied. They had another four hours to go before getting to the Comox base. From Comox, they'd be flying to Seattle and onto Kandahar from there. They needed to sleep now. When they arrived in Kandahar, there was no knowing when they'd get their next chance.

Diana glanced out of the window. She couldn't help a small sigh. The Canadian countryside was beautiful. So green and lush, so alive. So different from the poverty-stricken, war-torn dust bowl they were heading to.

CHAPTER THREE

"SIR, MA'AM, WE'RE nearly there," a voice said, waking Diana and Peter up. They were alert instantly, both of them experienced in moving at will from a state of sleep to one of vigilance.

"Thank you, Lieutenant," Peter said, his voice clear and quick.

Diana looked out. If you'd seen one military base, you'd seen them all: guard posts, high fences, and everything a dull gray. It wasn't an architect's dream, but it did lend a degree of familiarity and comfort.

At the gate, after verifying their credentials, they were waved through. The SUV pulled up in front of a low-rise building.

"General Edwards is expecting you," the lieutenant said.

"Thanks for the ride, Lieutenant Mizota, Corporal Jones," Diana said.

"Yeah, thanks," Peter added.

The corporal got their bags out of the trunk. "Good luck

over there, Captain, Major," Mizota said with a salute. Diana and Peter saluted back.

Peter knew better than to help Diana with her bag, but it grated a little, and he said so. "We're not civilians now," she reminded him. "Women have a tough time in the army as it is. I'm quite capable of carrying my bags."

Peter nodded with a grunt, and together they strode into the building. After speaking to another corporal, they were shown to the base commander's office.

"Major Peter Hopkinson, Canadian Special Forces, reporting for duty, sir!" Peter saluted.

"Captain Diana Hunter, INT, reporting for duty, sir!"

The commander looked to be in his early fifties. His close-cropped, gray hair had brown dotted through it. He looked a bit like Donaldson in many respects. They shared the same bulldog countenance. But where Donaldson was a little soft around the middle, this man was a soldier through and through, a wall of solid muscle.

"General Christopher Edwards," the man responded with a salute. "Welcome to CFB Comox. At ease. So, I understand you're getting a lift to a US Army base outside Seattle."

"Yes, sir. We'll be hitching a ride with the Americans to Kandahar from there," Peter said.

The general nodded. "I haven't been informed of the particulars of your mission." Edwards looked rather annoyed. In Diana's experience, generals thought they should know everything, but being one didn't automatically mean receiving security clearance for every op. More than once, Diana had known base commanders attempt to get more information by putting lower-ranking officers on the spot. The general seemed to be doing that now.

Diana cleared her throat. "Unfortunately, General,

we're in the dark too, sir. We received orders to get to Kandahar and were told we'd be briefed on the ground."

Peter threw her a look that she ignored. The general grunted. "Just like INT to pull something like this. Well, I'm still surprised. You've both been out of service for a while now. We have more than capable people on *active* duty."

"There must be a reason for it, sir," Peter said quickly, glancing at Diana who gave the general a strained smile.

"I guess there is. Well, your flight leaves in thirty minutes, so you better get going."

They left the general's office and were escorted to the aircraft. As soon as they had boarded and settled in, Peter turned to Diana. "Why didn't you just tell him our mission was classified? You lied to a superior officer."

"I didn't exactly lie. We don't know why Lennox wants us there, do we? Besides, it's a lot easier to fudge the truth a little than to tell a general I have clearance that he doesn't."

"I guess you have a point."

Diana snorted. "You have no idea. Last time I tried to tell a general my mission was classified and he didn't have clearance to hear about it, he argued with me for over an hour. He seemed to think I was withholding some critical information that prevented him from doing his job when our plane was only stopping at his base to deliver supplies! I don't know about you, but I don't have the time to sit through a rant like that, and I certainly don't possess the patience." Diana shook her head and looked away. "Men," she said under her breath. Peter smiled to himself. Some things never changed.

Less than an hour later, they landed at the US Army base. This time, the base commander didn't fish or argue, he didn't even inquire as to their mission, and after a brief courtesy call, they were on their way again.

A C5 Galaxy, along with a squad of soldiers and a great deal of equipment, was to transport them to Kandahar, Afghanistan. They had a 15-hour flight ahead of them.

When most of the soldiers around them had fallen asleep, Peter turned to Diana. "So, I think it's time you tell me how you ended up a captain in the Canadian military?" he whispered. "I thought you were a CSIS agent, a magazine editor, a consultant to VPD, and before that a student and a child, perhaps even a baby at one time. What's the real deal?"

"I was all those things, but TFI is a military organization, and when I was transferred, they sent me to boot camp, basic officer training, and then to the Canadian Forces School of Military Intelligence for a few months."

"They made you a captain out of the gate?"

Diana shook her head. "No, I took part in some, shall we say, interesting missions, and I got promoted."

"Huh, unusual but impressive."

"Look who's talking, *Major*," Diana said with a wink.

Peter shrugged. "I was in for a lot longer than you." He looked at her out of the corner of his eye, his lips thinning before focusing ahead once more.

"I thought you weren't allowed to see my file." Diana had submitted Peter for CSIS clearance so she could tell him about her background.

"I'm not, and I haven't. But you know, friends. I got some highlights. You rescued the passengers from that hijacked plane in Lahore, didn't you?" Peter closed his eyes and gave the barest of nods. "There were 104 women and children on that plane. They all got out alive because of you and your men."

"Not all of them. One woman was killed before we got there."

"99% of them, then. Sheesh."

Four years earlier, a British Airways flight from London to Delhi had been hijacked by a terrorist group and diverted to Lahore in Pakistan. The women and children on the plane were removed and taken to a camp outside the city. The other passengers, the men, remained on the aircraft. After five days of fruitless negotiations and mounting tension, two teams simultaneously stormed the plane and the camp to free the hostages in a coordinated attack. Peter led the team that rescued the women and children.

Under the cover of darkness, Peter and his men had returned to the remote buildings over and over to ferry the hostages to waiting helicopters, killing or incapacitating their captors in the process. The group, holding mostly Indian and British nationals, had cruelly made the task much more difficult by separating the women from their children, placing them a quarter of a mile apart. Some women had to leave the camp without knowing if their children were safe. It had been an excruciating, painstaking operation requiring exquisite organization, finesse, and ruthless killer instincts in what was an emotionally fraught and delicate situation.

Peter stared straight ahead as Diana regarded his profile. "You were awarded the Canadian Victoria Cross!" she hissed.

Diana's reference to the medal, the highest honor to be awarded by the Canadian government, caused Peter to start. It was a tiny movement that he quickly quelled, but he knew Diana would notice. "You know how it is." Peter rubbed a hand over his face.

Peter's memory of the op wasn't as unabashedly positive

as Diana's understanding of it. He became antsy just thinking about it and usually firmly put his recollection of the night's events out of his mind whenever they threatened to intrude.

The Special Forces units had been aided in their mission by a local man who had infiltrated the camp a few days before the rescue. His name had been Hamid. He was in his early twenties, idealistic, in awe of the West, his knowledge gained via Instagram and YouTube. Tall and lanky, with wild, wiry, dark hair, Hamid had a mother and a twelve-year-old sister. His father had been killed by Pakistani insurgents a couple of years before.

Although he never said as much, it was likely that Hamid believed that in return for his help with the mission, he would be rewarded with refugee status and a passage to a friendly, developed country for himself and his family. Peter had always felt guilty about that, even though the point was moot in the end. The military was littered with stories of broken promises of safe passage to translators and other members of the local resistance and their families. There had been no guarantees for Hamid, but he had helped anyway.

It was Hamid's intelligence that enabled the units to map out the encampment to understand the locations of the hostages and the conditions in which they were held. The military teams were able to rehearse the drop, search, and rescue many times in preparation for the mission, thanks to Hamid's assistance. He had been essential to its ultimate success.

When they launched, the night had been dark, with no moon visible. Perfect conditions. The air was warm and deathly silent. There was no sound except for the odd rustle in the bushes. Four Chinooks dropped the soldiers two miles from the camp. Jeeps had been readied for transport. Twenty-five soldiers raced across the dust, guided only by nightlights. There was no talking, only unwavering concentration on what lay ahead, and the fortitude needed for the success of the mission. A quarter mile from the camp, the jeeps split up to take up positions from where they would commence their assault.

As planned, the teams surrounded the outside of the camp, and in three waves, they repatriated the hostages. The first wave killed or neutralized the captors; the second invaded the buildings and released the women and children as the camp was secured. The backup unit dispatched the hostages back to the helicopters that were waiting for them. The strategy had worked like clockwork. Almost.

CHAPTER FOUR

PETER DROVE THE final hostages to the last helicopter. Hamid was with him. In Peter's ear, he heard a message from control.

"We count 97 hostages, sir." Peter's heart missed a beat.

"Give me a breakdown. Over."

"50 adults; 47 children. Over." 103 hostages had been taken to the camp, 52 women and 51 children. Peter had two women and three children sitting behind him. *He was missing a child.*

The voice came over his earpiece again. "A boy, we think, three years old."

Peter skidded the jeep to a stop, dust flying over his passengers as he braked.

"Hamid, take over. Drive like hell to the transport." The young man dipped his head in agreement.

"What are you going to do?"

"Right now, I'm going to find a child. After that, I'm not sure. Hang on as long as you can, but don't jeopardize the safety of the others. Leave if you have to." Peter jumped out of the jeep. Hamid roared off.

Peter ran back to the camp and went building to building, searching every room, alternately shouting and listening for sounds. He saw and heard no movement or noise. Then as he rounded a corner of the third building, a whine of gunfire sounded and chips blasted off the stone wall next to his head as a volley of shots flew through the air.

Damn! Peter raised his gun and fired into the night. A rogue fighter responded, and a gunfight ensued as Peter desperately tried to quell the threat quickly. Under fire, ducking and covering, he continued to search for the boy, moving between buildings. Frustrated, he looked around in the dark. He was wasting precious minutes defending himself against the insurgent, but despite his night goggles, he couldn't see his enemy.

A movement in his peripheral vision caught Peter's eye as he pressed forward. A man ran between a burned-out chassis and a building. He hobbled, obviously injured, but he was able to slip behind a wall. As the man continued to fire shots into the air, Peter held his ground, waiting for the gunman to reload. At the inevitable pause, Peter quickly crept forward, rounded the corner of the building, and fired a volley of shots into it. He waited again. There was silence. Peter entered the building, still covering, but after stepping over the body of the man, he resumed his search for the boy.

The final building was empty. When he resurfaced, wondering where to search next, Peter considered the bush around the camp. Maybe the boy had run.

It was nearing dawn. The darkness was lifting. If the child had fled, finding him would require an air search. That was too risky in daylight, and by evening, the boy would be dead. The heat would kill him. Peter swore as he prepared to radio the waiting Chinook. He would stay. If he found the child, he could keep him alive until a rescue was mounted for them both.

Peter crouched and faced a wall to send his message. He heard a noise. It came from rocks stacked into a makeshift box, two-foot square, and covered with a cement slab. A grain store. There was an opening on one side close to the ground. Peter kneeled down but immediately dove for cover as a bullet ricocheted off the cement block. Peter fired into the dark and heard a thud. He waited. Nothing.

Peter leaned into the opening in the pile of rocks and shone his flashlight inside. Two young, dark eyes looked back at him. Gripped by a force that bordered on panic, Peter ripped off the cement slab and grabbed the boy. On the horizon, the sky was turning gray. He started running. Two miles. Two miles back to the helicopter transport. He radioed control.

"Hostage retrieved. Returning to base. Over."

"Still here, sir. We have to leave soon. Hurry. Over."

Peter cradled the silent, traumatized boy in his arms. He didn't struggle but got heavier as Peter covered the ground. He shifted the boy's position, swinging him around and placing his head against his shoulder, the boy's body clutched to Peter's chest. As he ran, panting, the boy's body getting heavier with every stride, Peter worried. There was only bush around them and the darkness of the night sky continued to fade. Shortly, they and the helicopter would be exposed. The Chinook couldn't wait much longer.

Peter broke cover as the desert around him opened up, the bush taking a break. Up ahead, he saw the shadow of a vehicle coming toward him. He ducked instantly. The lights were off, but Peter could see Hamid at the wheel, his *shemagh* wound around his head, covering his nose and mouth as the desert dust blew all around him. Hamid had come back for them!

Peter stood and waved. Hamid pulled up, braking sharply. Peter clambered in with the boy still pressed against his body, and they raced to the waiting chopper, its blades spinning, anxious to leave.

Peter clambered aboard, the boy snatched from him by his terrified mother, but as he turned to close the doors of the aircraft, he found Hamid still on the ground. The young man stood looking up at him, a beacon of calm among the chaos of dust and sand barreling around just downwind of the spinning propellers.

"Get in! We have to leave now!" Hamid shook his head, the helicopter blades drowning out his words. He crossed his wrists, his fists at his chest in salute. "Get in, man. Now!" Peter desperately looked behind him at the pilot awaiting his order. He leaned over and held out his hand to Hamid, urging him forward, but Hamid didn't move, a rueful smile flickering across his lips. Even now, Peter didn't know why. Pride, loyalty, a refusal to leave his family, who knew? Hamid, for his traitorous help, faced certain death.

A shout came up from the cockpit. It was nearly light. They couldn't wait a moment longer. Peter sat at the open door of the Chinook, depleted and helpless, and gave the command to lift off. As he watched Hamid's upturned face diminish as the helicopter rose into the air, Peter beat his chest twice with the side of his fist and slid his open palm sideways from left to right. He acknowledged Hamid as his equal, his brother-in-arms, thanking him for his help.

The helicopter blades dipped and the chopper swooped away. Still watching from the open door, Peter put his head in his hands as below, clouds of dust kicked up. Insurgent's jeeps raced across the desert and the pulse of automatic gunfire punctuated the air. Hamid's body was recovered two days later.

On his return home, Peter negotiated safe passage for Hamid's mother and sister to a Northern European country. He also recommended Hamid for a civilian honor, stressing the unlikelihood of Peter's and the boy's survival had Hamid not risked his life to return for them. Instead, Peter found, to his horror, himself nominated for a Victoria Cross, an award he had accepted but felt embarrassed by and unworthy of.

Now, sitting next to Diana in another military transport but under quite different circumstances, he shrugged again. "Just doing my job," he said.

Diana snorted. "If everyone did their jobs like that, we'd need an army a quarter of the size it is now." Peter didn't respond. They fell into a long silence.

Eventually, it was Peter's turn to go on the offensive, and he was anxious to change the subject. "So, you said you'd tell me about you and that Inglewood guy," he said.

"Another time," Diana replied, inclining her head toward the soldiers who were awake. "Let's just say Clive was wrong on several occasions and I was right, but because I was younger, and possibly because I am a woman, he refused to listen to me. He ended up blowing a few ops and getting reprimands. He only got the job he has now because I turned it down."

Clive Inglewood was the Assistant Director of Intelligence at CSIS. Peter had met him two days prior during a briefing. Inglewood's dislike of Diana had been obvious. The temperature of the room had dropped to glacial levels when he'd arrived.

"Wow, bet he loves you," Peter said.

Diana sighed. "I guess so, though I never did anything

on purpose to antagonize him or to show him up. He just never listened to a word I said. According to him, I was an 'inexperienced child who didn't know her ass from her elbow.'"

"Well, obviously he's an idiot."

Diana gave Peter a regretful smile. "It was annoying at the time, but what's worse is that we suffered casualties because he was so thick-headed." Diana paused, thinking. "But who knows, maybe it would have been the same had I been in charge."

"Then how come he got promoted? I'd have thought blown ops, reprimands, and casualties would be enough to disqualify him from the start."

"I'm guessing he had some powerful friends. I know Amanda would have never chosen him." Amanda Stone was CSIS's Deputy Director of Operations, and Diana's former boss and supporter.

"Hmph, politicians, no doubt. They should keep their noses out of things. It's asking for trouble, especially when it comes to an agency like that. Let's hope they figure it out before it's too late and we have our own 9/11."

"From your lips to God's ears," Diana said softly.

CHAPTER FIVE

P ETER BREATHED A sigh of relief when they
finally landed in Kandahar. He hated being cooped
up for so long. Unclipping his seat belt, he stood
and stretched, unwinding his muscles. "God, that feels
good," he said with an appreciative groan.

Peter and Diana grabbed their gear and headed for the
exit. It was toward the front. The plane's nose had been
raised to allow for the removal of the large cargo stowed in
the hold. The C-5 had a cargo deck that ran the entire
length of the airplane. Besides military passengers, it had
been transporting some heavy equipment to Kandahar.

Diana and Peter waited as two jeeps and three tanks
rolled down the ramp and off the plane. When they disembarked, they found Ethan Lennox and a corporal waiting on
the runway next to a well-worn jeep covered with sand.

"Diana!" Lennox exclaimed, opening up his arms.
Diana ran right to him. Peter looked on, bemused. Theirs
wasn't exactly a formal military greeting. What was it with
the men in Diana's past? Did they have to put their hands

all over her? That Lennox was looking as good as always pleased Peter even less.

Peter tamped down the urge to fold his arms and tap his foot while he waited for Ethan and Diana to greet each other. He wondered again about Diana's background and what it was that seemed to incite such reverence and affection in those with whom she'd worked. It was unusual and ran counter to the low-key culture of the military and intelligence services. Receiving a landing strip welcome from the head of TFI was extraordinary.

"It's good to see you, Ethan," Diana said.

Lennox tucked her under his arm and grinned at Peter. "Good to see you, Hopkinson. Glad you could join us. Welcome to the stiflingly hot dust bowl that is Kandahar, but you know that already." Lennox extended a hand. Peter took it, unwilling to let his insecurities affect his relationship with the head of TFI.

"Glad to be here," Peter said, a little too curtly. He hoped his tone would pass for military formality.

"This is more of a welcome than we expected. I'm surprised you came yourself," Diana said to Lennox.

"Had to come see my favorite operative now, didn't I?" Lennox said with a grin. He was as smooth as ever. If Peter didn't know better, he'd say the man was a ten out of ten. But no one was perfect.

Diana laughed. "As big a charmer as always."

Lennox grinned, his eyes twinkling. "Glad you think so." Diana smiled back at him.

"Shouldn't we get going?" Peter asked, intent on breaking up this lovey-dovey reunion.

Lennox sobered instantly. "You're right. We have a lot to discuss and very little time in which to do it."

They all piled into the jeep, and somehow, Peter ended

up sitting in front with Corporal Brian Hollings. Lennox sat in the back with Diana. They spent most of the ride speaking quietly, which irritated Peter even more. They were chatting like the old friends they were. He felt bested by Lennox and excluded by Diana.

Peter decided to focus his attention elsewhere. Kandahar was just as he remembered. It was a scrappy city, full of poverty and dust, and was ridiculously hot. Low-rise buildings, the architecture of which suggested they were built in the seventies, interrupted rows of ordinary but decrepit, broken-down homes—more like huts if Peter were honest. Every building bore the scars of war.

Bullet holes peppered walls. Some were missing entirely, thanks to the IEDs, missiles, and other explosive devices that had rained down upon the city in recent years. Many buildings were now simply piles of rubble, while others had been abandoned. Some still fulfilled the objective of providing shelter, but barely.

Outside many of them, wrinkled clothing hung from desultory lines, the occasional toy and the debris of life scattered across the gritty, pitted ground. Every twenty yards or so, armed soldiers milled about on guard duty, patrolling, attempting to keep the area secure and the residents safe.

Despite the constant threat of danger, the streets were full of people going about their business. Many were on their way to the market, walking dolefully, or unevenly peddling on cranky bicycles. Children played at the roadside, their innocence like a shoot of green in an expansive but otherwise barren desert. Peter hadn't missed it one little bit.

He tried to relax, bumping up and down in his seat as the jeep's suspension proved no match for the uneven road surface, but his skin prickled. Danger. He looked around, searching for the source of the feeling, but saw nothing.

Then, he heard it. A whoosh followed by a whine and a rush of air. Peter knew in an instant exactly what it was. "Get down!" he yelled before the ground in front of the jeep exploded in a flurry of dust and rock.

CHAPTER SIX

PETER HUNG IN midair, suspended by his seatbelt when he came to. The air was still and silent. He looked about moving just his eyeballs as he took in the scene around him. The jeep had tipped on its side. Beneath him, Peter saw their driver, his lower body trapped under the vehicle, blood trickling from a head wound. The corporal was dead.

Peter turned to look in the back of the jeep, but his belt trapped him. He checked his arms and legs for injury, then braced himself against the dashboard and the seat and pressed the seatbelt's release button. It worked, and he fell from the seatbelt's clutches. He twisted awkwardly to view the back seat, but it was empty. He scrambled to look in the foot well, then to the ground where the jeep had turned over. There was no sign of Diana or Lennox. Their seatbelts dangled uselessly over the back of the seat.

Peter scrambled quickly to leverage himself out of the jeep. He could hear sounds of life as others in the vicinity started to move, checking themselves and those around them. A wail rose into the dusty sky and reached his ears. Peter winced. He knew that wail and what it meant.

He jumped down and scuttled around the back of the jeep. Lennox had been thrown ten feet from the vehicle. He was lying on his side, his back to Peter, and as Peter looked, he saw Lennox's prone figure stir. He was alive, he'd be alright. Now, to find Diana.

Peter contemplated the idea that he had been pushing away, that Diana was under the jeep. He ran all around it, but there was no sign of her. *Where was she?*

He looked up, scanning his surroundings. What was now half a two-story house stood to his left. The right side was missing; the downstairs rooms were exposed. A chair was upturned against one of the remaining walls and remnants of a meal lay on the floor. Rubble was strewn on the ground outside the house and across the road, but a low wall separating the front of the building from the thoroughfare was still intact.

He watched as a dusty toddler, mute from shock staggered from the house and over to the wall. The child bent down and as he did so, a hand appeared and clutched the top of the wall. A female hand.

"Mama," the child called out in Farsi. The toddler ran back inside the house where a woman stood, leaning against the doorjamb with her eyes closed, rubbing her face with her hand. Peter wordlessly ran over and helped Diana up, scanning her for signs of injury.

"I'm okay, I'm okay," she said. "You?"

"I'm fine. "

"What about Lennox?"

"He's over there."

As they turned to look, they saw Lennox slowly getting to his feet, quickening his movements as his mind cleared and the ongoing danger of their situation penetrated.

"Sit here," Peter said, helping Diana onto the wall. He ran to Lennox. "We need to get out of here."

Lennox stared at him. The older man blinked and looked around him. "We're not far."

Peter nodded back toward the jeep. "Your driver . . ."

Lennox lumbered over and inspected the body. "I'll send my people to get him." He reached over and pulled a pistol from the dead man's holster and threw it to Peter. "Just in case you need it." He checked to make sure his own was still in place. "The radios aren't working. Where's Diana?"

"I'm here." Diana levered herself off the low wall and walked up to them, a little unsteadily. Veiled in dust and with a trickle of blood running across her forehead from a cut in her hair, she was doing her best to be all business. Peter put an arm around her waist and pulled her against him. She leaned in for support.

"Follow me," Lennox said.

For the next half hour, they skirted the myriad alleyways and side streets of Kandahar. As they got further from the point of the explosion, the scene around them normalized. Men on bicycles zig-zagged in and out of crowds of women carrying shopping and babies. Children played in the streets. These were people used to warfare. Bombings, shootings, disruption, and threats were part of their daily life. Practiced in quickly picking up their lives after an event, they restored their routines rapidly, before resuming almost as if nothing had happened. Resiliency was the key to survival in Kandahar.

Lennox led Diana and Peter quickly and silently between buildings, keeping them away from the main thoroughfares and marketplaces. The heat was stifling. Their lungs hurt from the blast but Diana and Peter kept up with Lennox, unwilling to be separated or slow their journey down.

Eventually, they arrived in front of a small home. At Peter's quizzical look, Diana pursed her lips and closed her eyes, shaking her head minutely. Peter looked back at the house.

"House" was a stretch. A mud hut would be a more accurate description. In front, a lopsided wooden door hung —barely—on its hinges. The wood looked rotten. The windows were tiny, mere holes cut into the walls with wooden shutters hung on either side, green paint flaking off them. At some point, the structure had come under attack. It was liberally sprinkled with bullet holes.

"It's more impressive on the inside," Lennox assured him.

"I hope so. I've been expecting big things," Peter said.

Once they walked through the front door, though, Peter was disappointed. An old couch with faded upholstery sat against one wall. A chipped wooden coffee table stood in front of the couch, and a battered armchair with broken springs sat off to the side. In the corner was a larger table with three mismatched chairs around it. A plush purple cushion lay on the floor.

Against the opposite wall, there was a TV that had to be forty years old. It sat on a cupboard originally painted mustard but now faded and chipped. An elderly man and a woman wearing traditional garb sat on the worn and shabby sofa watching the TV intently, its fuzzy picture shuddering every few seconds. They didn't look up when the trio walked in.

Lennox walked straight through the living room and

into a tiny kitchen. Diana and Peter followed him. The three of them could barely fit within its walls. Lennox pulled out his phone and tapped something on the screen. One of the cupboard doors slid open. Inside was a biometric scanner. After it had scanned Lennox's eye and his fingerprint, he made an announcement. "Shearing sheep can be painful if you don't move fast."

There was a click, and the back wall slid aside to reveal a metal door. With a quiet whoosh, the door glided open to reveal an elevator. "After you," Lennox said to Diana.

Diana got in. Lennox walked into the large metal box, followed by Peter who was now much more impressed.

"Shearing sheep? Really?" he said.

"Not my idea," Lennox replied.

Lennox hit a button, and the elevator began to descend. After a while and quite a distance, it opened to reveal a small hall. Ahead of them, there was another heavy metal door that looked like that of a bank vault. An eye and fingerprint scan and another wild-ass phrase later—Peter had to wonder about the person who made Lennox say things like, "Aardvarks love eating ants in spring"—and the door opened. It not only looked like the opening to a bank vault but was as thick as one. A missile was unlikely to dent it. What Peter saw as he walked through the door did impress him. A lot.

CHAPTER SEVEN

L ENNOX TURNED TO them. "Let's get a medic
to look at your head wound, Diana. You too,
Peter."

Diana waved him away. "I'm fine. We need to get started." Lennox looked inquiringly at Peter.

"Me too. Fine."

"Okay, I have to communicate news of the casualty.
Give me a moment." Lennox walked away.

Peter looked around as he and Diana strolled along a
platform suspended above a room of at least 50,000 square
feet. Below them spread rows of computers. Operators
worked calmly and seriously at them. It looked like a
massive NASA control room. If not for the military
uniforms, Peter would have suspected he was inside mission
control. Lennox reappeared and watched Peter expectantly.

"Okay, I'm impressed," Peter acknowledged,
grudgingly.

"You weren't sure, were you?"

"No. No, I wasn't. But now I am," Peter replied.

"We have over three million square feet of space down

here, and that doesn't include the vehicle parking lot, the hangar, or the personnel quarters. Everything is connected by tunnels. The personnel quarters are about a mile to the east, while the parking lot and the hangar are next to each other, about 15 miles northwest. We've got a small electric monorail system for passengers and cargo."

"Hangar?" Peter asked.

"For choppers and planes."

"You've got fighters and helicopters down here?" Peter asked.

Lennox nodded. "The hangar is under a remote area of the desert. The helicopters can take off vertically through the hangar doors in the ceiling, the floor of the desert essentially, while a hydraulic platform lifts the planes out and cues them up with a runway on the surface."

"And no one has noticed a set of metal doors in the ground and a runway in the middle of the desert?"

Lennox grinned. "They might have, but they think it's all part of an abandoned airstrip."

Peter shook his head. "I feel like I'm in a movie. How did you build all this without anyone wondering what was going on?"

"It wasn't easy, and it took a while, but once it was decided Kandahar would be our main base of operation, we began work under the guise of a mining operation. Construction started in the desert. We dug down, hollowed out a cavern which is now the hangar, and built back toward the city, connecting to the house you saw upstairs. Since it was all done underground, we could conceal what we were doing. We brought in the larger equipment in pieces and assembled it down here to alleviate suspicion. It took four years to build this place, but it was well worth it."

Peter's eyes widened. "I can see why. How far down are we?"

"1.3 miles. The whole facility is encased in lead."

"Fast elevator," Peter commented. "I'm assuming the depth is to keep out prying eyes?"

"You are correct."

"But wouldn't, say, a Chinese or Russian spy satellite pick up a huge, unnaturally shaped block of lead wedged underground? All the straight lines and right angles?"

Lennox grinned. "That's one of the reasons it took so long to build this place. On the inside, the walls, floors, and ceilings are smooth and straight but the outside of the lead casing is jagged and uneven, mimicking the rock layer we cut into."

Peter shook his head. "You guys thought of everything, didn't you?"

At that point, Lennox grimaced. "Almost. We have one challenge. Bringing in supplies for the hundreds of people working down here can be complicated. That's why we've been considering expanding the facility to get some sort of food production going. A few greenhouses and maybe even some animals."

"Now you're kidding me," Peter said.

"Maybe," Lennox replied, looking guilelessly at Peter.

"You'd be self-sufficient if you did that. Hell, in the event of a nuclear war, you'd be completely safe and able to survive indefinitely," Diana said. Her eyes shone, her imagination alive.

Lennox nodded. "Exactly. This place was modeled, in part, on the plans of some nuclear bunkers the higher-ups are considering building. We just beat them to it."

Peter rocked on his heels. "Better to just avoid a nuclear war."

"I hear you, but, unfortunately, we don't have control over every Tom, Dick, and Harry with access to nuclear weapons. All it takes is for one nuclear warhead to hit the ground somewhere in the world, and the next thing you know, we'll have a full-scale war, even if it was just some crazy warlord launching the damn thing."

Peter sighed. "I know. MAD works fine between reasonable people; the mentally ill and suicidal, not so much. You said you had quarters down here too?"

"It takes a lot of people to run this place. We're the central hub for intel collection and analysis for all of Asia, Europe, and Africa. Add to that the number of agents and operatives we have, and someone would notice that many new people if they lived up there," he said, pointing to the ceiling.

"But being underground for so long—don't you have psychological issues?"

"Some people have a problem with it, certainly. We rotate them out every few months or so, but others have no problem at all."

"Well, if I hadn't seen it with my own eyes, I would have accused you of watching too many sci-fi movies."

"I'm glad you like it," Lennox said with a grin. "Unfortunately, we're on the clock, but once you've finished your task here, maybe Diana can show you around. I don't think anyone knows this base quite as well as she does."

CHAPTER EIGHT

"**I**S THAT SO?" Peter asked, turning to regard Diana who was concentrating on something that appeared to be happening past his head.

Lennox chuckled. "When Diana first got here, she made it her mission to inspect every last millimeter of the place."

Diana blushed and was forced to defend herself. "Hey, I was curious. This place is an incredible feat of engineering." Diana had kept quiet thus far, allowing Peter to take the TFI base in. She'd been in awe of it the first time she'd seen it, too. As Lennox said, she'd walked around in astonishment for the first few days, checking out the entire place.

"We frequently had to send people out looking for her. I think she just wanted to make sure the construction workers had done their jobs properly," Lennox whispered conspiratorially to Peter.

Diana glared at Lennox. He was patronizing her. "I was doing no such thing. I was fascinated, and I still am."

"Does that mean I'm going to have to drag you out of an air vent again?" Lennox teased.

Diana blushed again. "You never had to drag me out of an air vent," she huffed.

No, that was me. Peter thought back to that case. He'd had worse days.

Lennox snorted. "Probably the only place she didn't go. Alright, time is short, and we need to get you two briefed on what's been going on." He showed them into a glass-enclosed conference room with an enormous screen on the back wall.

Peter and Diana took a seat at the table. As at CSIS, the surface in front of them was a computer. Lennox typed on the tabletop and the large screen lit up ahead of them. It showed a map of Afghanistan on one side and Lucenzo Garibaldi's picture on the other. Garibaldi was the hitman whose headless body had been found in Vancouver, killed by The Surgeon before he could carry out the contracted hit on Canadian Senator Greene. Underneath Garibaldi's image, there were some notes.

"A few days ago, we heard chatter from ILIF that their man, Garibaldi, had failed in his mission," Lennox informed them. The Islamic Front, or ILIF for short, was a new fanatical group that had surfaced recently. Not much was known about them. "They were informed of said failure via a message that consisted of Garibaldi's head arriving on their doorstep."

Diana raised her eyebrows. "So, that's where it went."

"How did they get a head out of Canada and into Afghanistan without anyone noticing?" Peter wondered aloud.

"Forged paperwork to say it's for medical research or some kind of transplant?" Diana suggested.

"That's exactly what they did. Most customs agents

don't want to have anything to do with dismembered body parts," Lennox replied. "They gave it a wide berth."

"Okay, but why did this raise alarms for you? I mean, you guys deal with a lot more important stuff than a one-off hit on Canadian soil," Peter said.

Lennox nodded. "There is some evidence that this ties in with a more elaborate terror plot."

"What makes you say that?"

"As you know, Garibaldi's mission was to assassinate Senator Riley Greene," Lennox said. "But what we don't understand is why. What was this group of fanatics doing attempting to kill a Canadian politician? ILIF are new, unknowns. Seems a weird hit to start with."

"Kloch, the guy who ordered the hit on Garibaldi, told us it was because of Greene's policies. Apparently, he doesn't just want to keep troops in Afghanistan for peace-keeping and support, he wants to expand the Western military presence here. He's a hawk. That wouldn't make him very popular with ILIF," Peter said.

"Okay, let's run with that scenario. Let's say we take what Kloch says at face value. Greene hasn't announced his candidacy for Prime Minister. And there's no guarantee he'd win, right?" Lennox said. "Why kill him now? Why draw all this attention to themselves, and go to all this effort, for a politician who may not even get into power? Killing him now is way too premature."

"We thought the same when Kloch told us," Diana said. "Now, tell us something we don't know."

Diana was getting a little impatient. Touring the TFI underground headquarters was nice and all, but her head ached, and Afghanistan wasn't exactly what one would call a holiday destination. She and Peter hadn't come for fun so what had they been called there for? Lennox wouldn't have ordered them out to Kandahar for nothing.

"We have other intel that we've been looking into. We think that ILIF is planning something big. They may have cells operating in Canada already, possibly in the UK, US, France, and Germany, too."

"ILIF cells on the ground? I thought these guys were pretty new," Peter said.

"They are. And that's what's worrying. They've ramped up fast. We don't know who's involved with them yet, but—"

"You think they've got local support?" Diana said.

"Maybe. Something that looks kosher but isn't would be my guess." Lennox glanced at Diana, then Peter, a frown creasing his forehead. "What do you know about Kloch and his company, Blue Panther?" he asked them.

"We know Kloch ordered the contract on Garibaldi. He hired The Surgeon to do it, he says to protect Greene. He engineered the payment of $5 million to The Surgeon for the privilege. We were put under pressure to let Kloch go," Peter said.

"I've worked with Blue Panther before. They're good. Their men have given their lives to protect our troops. I don't want to jump the gun and accuse good men of being traitors," Lennox said.

Diana nodded. "I know. I doubt Kloch's men have anything to do with this. But Kloch was aggressive and evasive when we interviewed him. Helpful when we got him in a corner, but cagey and arrogant at the same time. Not entirely on the up and up."

"Hmm, okay let's table Kloch for now. I want more intel. That's why I asked you to come over. Di, we need your stealth, charm, and extraordinary superpowers." Lennox smiled as Diana's eyes narrowed. "There's an underground party happening tomorrow night. Someone we believe to be high up in ILIF will be in attendance. I want you to extract him."

"Okay, where? Not Afghanistan surely? I can't believe there are too many underground parties happening around these parts."

Lennox hesitated. "Dubai," he said finally.

"Dubai? But they're on board. Why did you need to bring us all the way here? You could do this," Diana waved her arm in the direction of the screen ahead of her, "with local operatives."

"Yeah, well, Dubai is on board, officially, politically, but when it comes to their territory, they're less inclined to let us come traipsing in and do as we please. We need to be quick, clinical, and above all, discreet. Things you are great at."

"You could have said something," Diana grumbled.

"Would it have made a difference?" Lennox asked.

Diana sighed. "No, but I might have brought some different clothes."

Lennox grinned. "All sorted. And yes, Versace, as always. I know how much you like their gear, even if I have no clue why anyone would pay $5,000 for a dress."

Diana snorted. "You are a complete caveman. It's not 'gear,' it's *haute couture*."

"And I'm pretty sure 'haute couture' means obscenely expensive in French."

Peter cleared his throat and folded his arms across his chest. "You want to send Diana in to grab a known terrorist? Not on her own, surely?"

Lennox and Diana both looked at him, their pupils

widening in surprise. Peter's face hardened. In their banter, they'd completely forgotten he was there.

"You will be her date," Lennox said.

Peter opened his mouth, ready to argue then snapped it shut. "Good," he said simply.

"What do you want us to do exactly?" Diana asked.

"What you do best, of course. Extract him and get us the intel we need."

"You need me to interrogate him?" Diana sought to confirm.

"Well," Lennox winced and gave her a sheepish look.

Diana stared at him. "Are you kidding me?"

CHAPTER NINE

"I STILL DON'T understand why it's so important to use Diana?" Peter said. "You have this huge operation. Hundreds of people work here. Are you telling me you couldn't find one woman to go undercover to some posh party?" he said.

"We have plenty of female agents who are more than capable. However, I can count on one hand the number of them who can do what Diana does. None of them can pull it off as quickly," Lennox said. "Diana does a lot more than interrogate."

Peter raised his eyebrows and looked at her. Diana sighed. "I turn them into assets."

"How so?"

"They become double agents. They report back to us."

"How do you do that?"

Diana shrugged. "It depends on the target. I learn what drives them. It's not a big deal."

Lennox snorted. "Not a big deal? Please. Diana's managed to turn some of the most fanatical men I've come across. I have no idea how she does it, but she does."

Diana's face tightened. It was so brief that it was barely noticeable, but Peter had gotten used to paying close attention. He saw the slight grimace.

"So, who's our target, and how long do we have?" Diana said. Lennox hesitated. "Why do I suspect I'm not going to like your answer?" Diana added, her eyes narrowing.

"His name is Firat bin Rahid Al Omair," Lennox said.

"Al Omair? Related to Dubai's ruling family, I presume?"

Lennox winced. "He's the youngest son."

"And some big hotshot in ILIF?"

"It appears so. We haven't connected him directly to any terror plots, but he seems to be in charge of the money. Not only is his daddy rich, but he also has the gift of the gab and isn't half bad in the boardroom, either. He's only twenty-five, but he seems to have a knack for investing in tech startups and picking winners most of the time. He started when he was seventeen and has managed to build up a sizeable fortune of his own. Unfortunately, it seems he's putting a lot of that money at the disposal of ILIF," Lennox explained. "I'm hoping that, at the very least, we'll be able to find out what's going on with Greene and why they targeted him."

Diana looked at Lennox thoughtfully. "Something's not right. Firat doesn't seem the type to get involved with people like ILIF. He doesn't sound like a religious fanatic, so what's his angle? Why is he involved with them?"

"That's the problem. We don't know. His ideology has nothing in common with those nutcases. It's the exact opposite. He likes booze, he likes his girls in bikinis, and he likes parties."

"Explain to me again why you think he'd turn against ILIF?" Diana asked.

"Isn't his lifestyle clue enough? It's clear he doesn't believe in ILIF's core beliefs."

"And that, right there, is the problem," Diana said.

"What do you mean?" Lennox asked.

Peter intervened. "If he's not in it for the ideology, it means he has an ulterior motive and is probably a little more calculated and shrewd than you are giving him credit for." Lennox looked at Peter in surprise.

"Exactly what Peter said," Diana interjected. "My bet is this Firat kid is a lot smarter than you think. I'd suggest that he's after something, and he's using ILIF to get it. ILIF is a means to an end."

"So, you're saying he wouldn't make a good asset?" Lennox said.

Diana shook her head. "Not necessarily, but I can't tell from the intel we have right now. I'll evaluate on the ground, but I bet that he doesn't give a rat's ass about ILIF."

Lennox didn't look pleased. "Dangerous game," he muttered. "You can still try?" he said, not quite ready to give up on the idea.

Diana shrugged. "To turn him? How long do I have?"

"His people are used to him going on benders so you have 24 hours with him before someone notices he's missing."

"Are you serious? I can't turn him that quickly!" Diana looked at Lennox aghast. She trailed off at the closed look on Lennox's face. "No," she snapped.

"Diana, please . . ." Lennox tried to placate her but swallowed hard when she leveled a lethal stare at him.

Peter didn't like this one bit. There was history here. Whatever it was, it had Diana on edge. She was . . . horrified, terrified. She didn't look it, but he knew her. Diana was covering her fear with anger.

"I can't do it," she said adamantly. "I can't flip him in 24 hours. There's no way."

"Diana, you know you can," Lennox said.

"I *will* not," Diana ground out. "I told you I was done with that. And you promised—you *promised*—you'd never ask it of me again."

"We don't have a choice! We have to get this intel. It's vital!" Lennox exclaimed.

Diana took a deep breath. "What about putting pressure on his family?"

Lennox shook his head. "You know what they're like. They'll say yes to our faces and do the exact opposite, and we don't have the time to play games, or for diplomacy for that matter. Whatever's going to happen, it will happen soon. We don't have months to wait for our governments to grind their diplomatic gears." Diana gave Lennox a hard stare.

"Diana," Lennox said, a warning tone in his voice, "we need a man on the inside. Firat could be that man. Think of the stakes. We can't screw this up."

"You think I don't know that? Listen, I will *not* be involved in something like that again. Write me up. Lock me up. Fire me. Do whatever you want, but I will *not* do that ever again. For *anything*."

Diana slammed her fist against the table. Peter started in surprise. She rarely had violent outbursts. What the hell was going on? What had Diana been involved in? Some dodgy practices were acceptable in the desert, but they were kept hush-hush, and he'd never have thought Diana would be a party to them.

"Come on, you can do it, Diana. I know you. I've seen what you can do. You are my best agent. You're smart and impressive. No one holds a candle to you." Lennox wasn't giving up.

"No, Lennox. I've already said."

Lennox paced the room and turned to look at her mulish face. "Diana, this isn't like you. I thought you were better than this." Now he was trying to guilt her.

"It's because I'm better than *this* that I'm refusing to agree to your plan."

Diana knew she was treading a fine line. Dealing with a charge of insubordination would be a pain in the ass, but she also had Lennox over a barrel. He needed her more than she needed him at this point. And what he was proposing wasn't official.

"You can say what you like, Lennox, but I am not going down that road again. We do it my way or not at all." Diana faced off with Lennox who glared at her. "Well? Are you going to order me?"

"You know I won't authorize it," Lennox said softly.

"I see, so I'm supposed to do it as a favor, am I? I'm supposed to carry out your dirty work while you hold your hands up and deny all knowledge if we get found out. Thanks very much, Lennox! I'll get whatever intel we can to the best of my ability with the time and resources we have. But my rules, my decisions. That's the deal I'm offering. Take it or leave it."

Lennox knew he was defeated. He sighed and then nodded. "Alright. What do you need?"

"Scopolamine," Diana replied.

"You sure?"

"It's the quickest way. Scopolamine will get us the intel we need and allow us to evaluate Firat as an asset for the future. He'll show us his true face, his feelings, motives, his personality. I can evaluate his suitability as a double agent then, but the job of flipping him needs to be done by someone else, *if* I consider it a worthwhile proposition."

Peter intervened. "Look, Lennox, Diana's right. She's the expert, and this isn't the time. Let's get the intel we need, and once we have it, you make your decision about Firat. Using scopolamine means you get a second bite of the cherry should you need it. Firat won't remember a thing."

Lennox stared at them, holding his breath, his lips pressed into a grimace. He let out a long sigh. "Okay, do it your way. But if you don't get the intel we need, we will all be deep in the brown stuff." Diana picked up her bag.

Wearily, Lennox continued. "I've set aside two rooms for you here overnight. Everything you need for tomorrow will be delivered to you, including your covers. You'll play the part of a rich married couple looking for a good time. What you do from there, I don't care as long as you get what we need. Come back here in an hour for a formal briefing from my Chief Intelligence Officer." Diana and Peter nodded their agreement. "I'll organize transport to your quarters," Lennox said. He sharply turned on his heels and left the room.

Diana stood and walked over to the screen. Peter could see her trembling. She was miles away, caught up in her thoughts. He walked up behind her and put his hands on her shoulders. She flinched.

"It's just me," he whispered in her ear. Diana nodded but didn't say a word.

The door opened and closed. "There's a corporal outside who will take you to your quarters," Lennox said, cooler now.

Diana stepped away from Peter and regarded Lennox

squarely. He returned her gaze without blinking. "I expected more from you," she said simply.

"Diana, if I felt I had another choice, I'd have taken it."

Diana looked at him for another long moment, disappointment etched onto her features. "Let's go, Peter," she said.

CHAPTER TEN

DIANA AND PETER found the corporal outside the conference room and followed him onto the platform above the banks of computers. After a lengthy stroll through the cavernous space, they boarded a small monorail car. Peter had hoped to see more as they traveled through the underground complex, but it had been cleverly designed so that nothing could be seen from the tracks. They proceeded through enclosed, blank, concrete tunnels, access to which was obtained via secured and heavily vaulted doors. There was no view or landmarks, and ten minutes later, as they disembarked, Peter felt utterly disoriented.

As they let themselves into their rooms, Peter opened his mouth to say something, but the haunted look on Diana's face stopped him short. She hadn't said a word since they'd left Lennox's company. Diana looked up so that the biometric device outside her room could scan her, and then went inside, closing the door behind her quietly, her head down.

Peter sighed and raised his face. After the camera had

scanned him, he entered his quarters. He looked around. The room was small and spartan but comfortable enough. At least there was a bed. There was a door to the right. Opening it, he found a small en suite with a shower, just what he needed after the long trip. Maybe he'd have some brilliant insight into what had just happened while he was in it. "Not bad," he whispered. They must have been given some of the best rooms in the complex.

After his shower, Peter was back in uniform and feeling much better, although no flashes of genius had assailed him while under the steaming jets of water. He glanced up at the wall that separated his and Diana's rooms and considered his next move. They needed to discuss their plan of action. And Diana needed to get whatever was bugging her off her chest. If she didn't, she could lose focus on the mission.

Peter checked the time. He'd give Diana another ten minutes. The following day, they'd head out to Dubai, and it would be too late. Peter lay on the bed, pondering the whole situation. He'd never seen Diana quite so off-kilter or so disillusioned.

Peter had his own skeletons locked away. He didn't consider them often, but he forced himself to mull them now. They swirled about his head like water pounding a boat in a squally sea, making progress difficult, the journey unpleasant. He glanced at his watch again and pushed himself upright, swinging his legs over the side of the bed. He got to his feet. It was time to check in with Diana.

Diana sat, blindly staring at the door to her en suite. She'd also taken a shower, not allowing herself to sink into inactivity and depression. She couldn't afford to. Not now. Not when they had a mission to accomplish. Diana wanted to slap Lennox for putting her in a bind, but she should have expected it. This was TFI, and this was their typical MO. They were famous for getting results any how, any way. But she'd thought, hoped, that Lennox wouldn't push her. They had worked together closely in the past, and he'd always seemed a good guy.

A knock on the door made Diana jump. She took a deep breath, bringing herself back to the present. Opening the door hesitantly, she found Peter standing in the doorway, looking at her with concern on his face.

"Are you okay?" he asked.

Diana considered her options quickly. She knew she could brush it off and play tough. But this was Peter. He'd never pull a stunt like Lennox.

Diana looked at him and made her decision. She shook her head slowly. "No, I'm not," she whispered.

"Do you want to talk about it?"

Diana shook her head again. She didn't want to remember those times, let alone talk about them. "No," she whispered again.

Peter swallowed hard and took a step back. He was hurt. That was the last thing she wanted. But her memories were too painful and shameful.

"Okay," he said with a sigh. He turned to leave.

"Don't go," she said quickly. "Stay. Let's talk about something else. Please." She reached out to grab his hand.

"Of course." Peter turned to face her again, his eyes warm.

Diana stepped back, giving him the space to enter her room, and closed the door. She turned to him. Her eyes widened. He pretty much filled up the small room.

Peter gave her a searching look. "You okay with what we have to do?"

Diana nodded. "I think so." She paused, her resolve melting. "I'd be more okay if I could come up with a method of flipping Firat that doesn't employ the techniques Lennox wants me to use." Diana laughed awkwardly. "I can't believe he asked this of us!"

"What is this 'this,' Diana? I think you need to tell me."

"Let's sit." Diana sank to the bed, and Peter took a beige molded seat facing her. He leaned forward. She took a deep breath and closed her eyes, placing her hands between her knees. Peter waited patiently.

"Whatever the problem is, you're not alone in this. It's okay," he whispered to her.

Diana's eyes opened, and she knew he'd see the tears she was doing her best to hold back. She gave him a wobbly smile. "I know," she whispered. She drew in another deep breath. "I don't want you to think I'm some neurotic, emotional twit who can't do what's required."

Peter barked a laugh. "Diana, neurotic and emotional are not words I would ever associate with you."

Diana's shoulders dropped, and she gave him a small, pained smile. "This 'this': I don't want to talk about it." She lifted her heels and rapidly bounced them up and down. Peter dropped his chin, waiting for her to speak. She looked away at the wall to her left, thinking, before sighing and looking down at the ground.

"When I first started at CSIS, they wanted to use my people-reading skills with suspected terrorists, people implicated in hate crimes, those who had made threats or were suspected of having been radicalized. I helped them in the interrogation room, to interpret what was going on. I would sit behind a two-way and talk to the interrogator via a headset. Using my feedback in real-time, we could usually steer the interviews to a successful conclusion. It worked pretty well. It was only when I got into the field that I realized interrogation tactics weren't quite as clean as they were at home. Questionable practices were common. Still, I was good enough to get the answers we needed quickly without having to go there. I was proud of what I achieved and how I achieved it. I felt I stayed on the right side of the line. And still got results.

"That's when I began to think. We were interrogating all these terrorists, extracting information from them, then imprisoning them, shoving them down a black hole where they would never see the light of day again. They're a wasted resource like that.

"I thought, what if we were to use them? What if we could turn them? Make them our asset? What if I developed a system to turn them into assets quickly and efficiently? Up to that point, there was no active strategy to develop or exploit them any further. I thought there was a way to get more return on our investment beyond the initial intel." Diana paused.

Peter kept quiet, allowing her to set the pace, for which Diana was grateful. Part of her was ashamed of what she'd done, but a big part of her was afraid to see the look in Peter's eyes when he discovered what she'd been a part of, what she'd gone along with. Peter was as straight as a die. It was one of the things she loved about him. He had no "side."

Diana took a deep breath and forged ahead. "Of course, the higher-ups at CSIS thought it was a brilliant idea. We'd have people on the inside without having to risk our own.

"They told me to develop a method that anyone could apply, so I did. It involved using various psychological strategies and triggers, including creating dependence and a mild form of capture bonding. We were dealing with fanatics who'd already been brainwashed, so I had to deprogram and then reprogram them again along the lines that would work for our purposes.

"I tested my theory and tweaked the practices until I got positive results 75% of the time. Once implemented, though, complaints came in from the field that it was taking too long. And their turn rate wasn't as good as mine. When I did it, I modified my strategy as I went along, taking my cues from the subject and adapting on the fly. That was a lot harder for others." Peter sat back in his chair and crossed his arms. Diana pressed on.

"So, they demanded I develop a foolproof method that yielded results quickly. This time, they had me work with a team of psychologists and interrogators, some of whom had applied my methods in the field. We worked together to adapt my program." Diana let out a big sigh. "Anyway, I was young, and I guess I let them overwhelm me because, by the time we were done, my approach had been corrupted. They incorporated blatant physical and mental torture practices to get results.

"When it rolled out, the results were much better, and my bosses were ecstatic. And this is the thing, I lapped it all up. I had no clue what they were doing at first, but in time I found out. They gave me the credit, and I think I was so full of myself and enjoyed being in the spotlight so much that I went along with it. It's a lot easier to convince yourself that something like that is okay when it's just a theoretical concept, and you don't see the action or take part in it.

"It was a while before I saw my program in the flesh. But then I was put in charge of the program in Kosovo. I had to do the dirty work. I never did any of the actual torturing, not the physical part, at least, but I was the one who took advantage of it. I was the 'good guy' on the tag team, the kind, empathetic one. The subject would bond to me to the point where they were willing to do anything I asked as long as I didn't abandon them. And I quickly reconciled myself to it. I was complicit."

Peter shifted in his seat, his arms still folded. Diana had looked down at the floor while she spoke. She hadn't dared look up at him. She didn't want to see what she feared in his eyes, the recrimination or the disgust. "With every person we turned, I'd lose another little piece of my soul. I kept telling myself it was for the greater good, that we were saving lives. The intel we got was invaluable, and we stopped many attacks. But at the same time, I kept asking myself, where should I draw the line? If I was willing to stoop so low, was I any better than the people we were fighting?

"One day, they put a sixteen-year-old boy in front of me who'd been kidnapped as a child and radicalized. He was a runner for a terrorist leader. He was so easy to turn. A few hours with the operative I was partnered with, and the boy cried when I left the room, begging and pleading with me not to leave him.

"That was the final straw. I told them that either they did things my way, or I'd walk. CSIS just figured I was having a breakdown, that I had spent too much time in the field, so they brought me back to Canada and stuck me behind a desk. I was getting ready to hand in my resignation when I transferred to TFI." Diana paused for a moment as she considered the memory. "When I got here, Lennox had been fully briefed on what I had done, and was, of course, interested in implementing the program. But he was smart. He told me that as long as I got results, he'd let me call the shots. He said he'd never force me to do something I wasn't willing to do. He never has, up until now. And I was grateful."

Diana closed her mouth with an audible click and finally looked up. She waited for Peter's reaction. His sky-blue eyes were icy.

CHAPTER ELEVEN

THE MOMENTS TICKED by, one after the other. Diana looked down again until she heard Peter let out a long sigh and then the sound of his voice.

"You know, this is war. It's an ugly, dirty, inhumane business. The decisions are tough, and it's rare to get results without some kind of collateral damage. Sometimes, we get carried away and forget what we're fighting for."

"I know, but still . . ."

"Listen, I've seen people do terrible things in a war zone. Things they would never do in their regular lives. When all our touch points, the people and places we love and are connected to, are missing, we lose ourselves. We become people we are not, especially if our environment is corrupted."

"But there's no excuse. I know all that, and I still went along with it—"

"Diana, you need to stop this. I don't blame you. I know you're a good person and that you'd have done things differently if you could. And I can't tell you how proud I am that you ultimately found the courage to say no. I know how difficult it is to stand up for what you believe is right, especially to people in an organization you are trained to obey."

"Did you ever compromise yourself?" Diana asked.

Peter held her gaze. "Not exactly."

"So why did I?" Her words came out as a wail.

"You were young. You were groomed."

"Yes, but, oh, I don't know." Diana started to cry. She placed both palms over her eyes and sobbed hard, bending over, her face on her knees.

Peter moved over to sit next to her. He took her in his arms, his lips pressed against the top of her head as she cried. They stayed like that for a long time. Eventually, the tears subsided. Diana looked up and dared a glance at him.

"Do you blame me?"

"No, I don't blame you." Peter had picked up her hand and, with his thumb, was thoughtfully rubbing circles into her palm. Diana had not known how relaxing and soothing a small gesture like that could be.

"You don't despise me?" she asked in a small voice.

Peter frowned and shook his head. "Of course not. How could I? You were doing your best to help and contribute to national and *inter*national security. If *we* can't get a break, who can?"

"Thank you," Diana whispered.

Peter frowned again. "What for?"

"For not condemning me," Diana said, wiping her cheeks with the back of her hand. "I feel so ashamed. Ugh. Sorry for being such a wimp." She got up to grab a tissue.

"Diana, a wimp you are not. But I have one question. How did I fit into Lennox's plan?"

"What do you mean?"

"Well, you said something along the lines of how could Lennox ask this of *us*, so I'm assuming I had a role to play."

Diana dipped her chin and looked at him from under her lashes. "He expected you to be the bad guy."

Peter's features remained impassive. "I see. I can't say I'm surprised, but I don't appreciate the assumption."

"I think Lennox is a good man, but he deals at the sharp end. Sometimes he forgets that some of us aren't willing to do what he thinks is necessary to get the job done. When I first met him three years ago, he was adamantly against the program in the form it was. He *said* he believed that the ends didn't always justify the means. It would appear he's changed his mind."

"He has a reputation for looking the other way at times. I understand that. The ends can justify the means if the threat is sufficient and there are no other options. But overriding the conscience of an operative is never a winning strategy. Tell me more about what you did. How did it work exactly?"

"It involved psychological torment."

"Like what?"

"Well, there are certain things we're all afraid of. We can't help it. Like being buried alive. My system involved making our captives believe their worst nightmares were coming true, though everything was completely simulated. Then I'd come in and make it stop every once in a while until they began to see me as their savior. In the end, they were willing to listen to whatever I had to say and do whatever I asked."

Peter looked at her. She could almost see the wheels in his head turning. "So, at no point were they in actual danger or subjected to any form of physical torture?"

Diana waggled her head from side to side. "Well, no,

not as I originally planned it, but sometimes. We took drastic approaches on occasion, especially with terrorists. In the few cases where we weren't dealing with a fanatic, I found a sweet enough carrot to dangle in front of them. That was usually enough, but if they were hardcore, we resorted to mind games in combination with physical threats. We'd go back and forth between psychological and physical 'motivators.'"

"How did you guarantee their long-term commitment? Didn't they just disappear or stop working for you once they were released back into their world?"

"That was the risk, which is why we kept meeting regularly—to remind them of their stake in what was going on. It was one of the reasons the brass at CSIS wanted a more permanent solution. It was expensive to keep bringing the assets in month after month. And to deliver on any incentives we'd promised them. I went into the field many times to make contact. It was a lot easier and cheaper to just beat the crap out of them and scare them into submission. A few reminders here and there kept them on our side. And their bond with me extracted the goods."

"So, what do you think you can work with this Firat guy?" Peter said.

Diana sat up straight now. She was on safer ground. "We'll use the scopolamine basically as a truth serum to get the intel we want. It's not sophisticated or clever, but it will get the job done. I'll evaluate Firat as a potential asset and leave it to Lennox to decide if he wants to take it further."

Peter nodded. "Alright, I'll follow your lead when it comes to getting the intel out of him. But that means you have to follow mine concerning getting in and out with our necks intact, okay?"

"It's not my first undercover mission, you know."

"Yes, I'm quite familiar with your undercover skills. I've had to get you out of trouble more than once, remember?"

Diana poked her tongue out at him. "They were flukes. And it still turned out fine, didn't it?"

"Yeah, but we were in Vancouver and had backup. Here, we're on our own. Just you and me, babe. And I think I have a little more experience with extraction jobs."

Diana was about to open her mouth to argue but thought better of it. She had nothing to prove to Peter. They were a team. And the sooner she started acting like it, the better off they'd both be. "Okay," she said.

"Okay?" Peter asked incredulously. "Not even a small, tiny argument? Not one sarcastic remark?"

"Keep talking, and I might change my mind," Diana said warningly, though a hint of a smile curled her lips.

"Watch you don't make me pull rank on you," Peter said with a grin.

Diana was outraged, sort of. "You wouldn't dare."

"Try me," Peter taunted.

He'd do it just to annoy her, she knew. "Well, you won't need to, because you're right."

Peter's eyes widened comically. "Now I know something's wrong. Giving in to me without a fight? Acknowledging my superior opinion on the matter? Are you the Diana Hunter I know? Or has some kind of alien invaded her body?" he said, his eyes narrowing.

Diana laughed. "I'm not that bad."

Peter lifted his eyebrows. "Really?"

"Fine, I may, sometimes, be slightly annoying. But it's only because I'm right. Most of the time, anyway."

Peter shook his head. "I knew it couldn't last."

Diana slapped him on the shoulder playfully. "Stop," she said. "You are impossible."

Peter grinned at her. "I know. You're not all sunshine and roses either, so we're a perfect match." Then he sobered. "So, we're going in as a couple, right?"

"That's our cover."

"And where are we supposed to perform this conversion miracle? In our hotel suite?"

"I guess so. Ideally, we'd bring Firat back here, but we can't risk taking him out of the country. Too dangerous and the authorities would notice."

"Will Lennox have cooked up some plan to get this guy out of the party or will he leave it up to us?"

Diana shrugged. "It's on us, specifically, you."

Peter raised a hand to his chest, placing it over his heart, as a shocked expression crossed his face. "Moi?"

"You're more than capable of coming up with something."

"Acknowledging my expertise *and* letting me take the lead twice in one day? Are you sure you're feeling alright?"

"Ha, ha. Aren't you the hilarious one?"

Just then, a knock sounded. Diana got up to answer and found the same corporal who'd escorted them to their rooms standing in the hallway.

"The Chief Intelligence Officer would like to speak to you and Major Hopkinson now, ma'am," he said.

Peter had already gotten to his feet. "Okay, let's get this party started." Peter stood back to let Diana through the door first. "After you."

CHAPTER TWELVE

I N THE EARLY afternoon, Diana and Peter arrived in Dubai on a luxury private jet. They'd played the part of the loving married couple from the moment they landed, but only just enough. Dubai might look cosmopolitan on the surface, but kissing in public is illegal, so they'd just held hands and stayed close to each other, maintaining appearances without going over the line.

When they learned they were staying in a suite at the Burj Al Arab Jumeirah, the distinctive sail-shaped hotel that had become a Dubai landmark, Peter's eyebrows climbed into his scalp. He'd thrown Diana a glance. She'd grinned at him. But they weren't staying there for fun. It was all about appearances. The party they were to attend was taking place in one of the hotel's penthouses.

As their limo drew up in front of the hotel, Peter prepared to pull his cover off. He wore a black suit with a white open-necked shirt. His shoes were highly polished. Aviator sunglasses peeked out of his jacket pocket. His brown hair was freshly cut and gelled in place.

Next to him, Diana was wearing a diaphanous dress

that draped and clung to her body, wrapping her in a print of cream and turquoise. Clunky, gold jewelry surrounded her neck and wrist. Huge earrings hung from her ears. She'd put her hair up in a messy ponytail, and a shocking pink Chanel purse hung from her wrist.

As soon as the car came to a stop, valets simultaneously opened their doors in an orchestrated maneuver. Peter swung out of the car in one elegant move, taking his sunglasses from his pocket and sliding them on. He needed them. The sun's glare was almost overwhelming and it wasn't much better inside the hotel. The place was lavish. Every surface shone. The couple didn't miss a beat, however. Their cover demanded that they act as though they stayed in places like this all the time.

All around them were white marble floors, plush carpets, and inviting couches. The ceiling dripped with glass teardrops, in between which were thousands of tiny lights that mimicked the starry sky. There was even a human-sized ornate teapot standing by one of the entrances. It added more than a touch of whimsy, although Peter didn't like it. There were so many colors and patterns. And they were all so bright.

When Diana and Peter got to their suite, they swept it for cameras and listening devices. Once they were confident it was clear, they relaxed. "Look at this place," Diana said.

Their suite was plush and luxurious. Peter flopped down on a couch and moaned with pleasure. "I could quite happily sit here for days if it wasn't for this color scheme threatening to give me a headache. I can't take my sunglasses off." Red, gold, yellow, and orange filled the room.

"I like it," Diana replied.

"You would." Peter got up and walked over to the

window. He looked out at the water below. "Ah, this is better." He stepped onto the balcony.

"What are you doing?" Diana called out.

"Giving my eyes a rest."

Peter checked his watch for the sixth time in five minutes, his eyes glued to the bathroom door. As he sat on the sofa in their suite, he fidgeted a little, pulling on the bow tie he was wearing. Damn thing made him feel as if he was choking. He was used to wearing bow ties, but it had been a while since he had. He got up and started pacing. What was taking Diana so long? She'd been in the bathroom for more than an hour.

He eyed the sumptuous comfort of the bed. He was sorry that he wouldn't get to try it out. It looked so inviting he was tempted to take a nap. He'd mess up his tux, though, and Diana would not be pleased, so he shut the thought down. But damn, that bed looked good.

Just then, the bathroom doorknob began to turn. Peter sat up straighter, curious to see how Diana would look. While his knowledge of fashion was practically non-existent, even he had heard of Versace.

Peter couldn't help but remember the last time he had seen Diana all done up. It had been at a gala where they'd again been undercover. He hadn't been able to get the picture of her in that dress out of his mind for weeks after the case. She'd looked stunning. That time, Diana had gone as a guest, and Peter had been a waiter. He much preferred his current, and equal, status.

Diana opened the bathroom door and Peter realized that, once again, her image would stick with him for quite some time. He immediately felt confused and unable to express himself with words that were anything other than monosyllabic.

Diana was wearing a frothy white and silver creation. A mass of white silk was stitched with tiny pearls at random and flecked with silver threads. The fabric followed the contours of Diana's slim body before sweeping out into multiple layers, some sheer, some not. They lay in waves that parted on one side to reveal an underskirt that peeked out from underneath and more calmly reached the floor. The bodice, strapless and fitted, nipped in at her waist. The uneven neckline was trimmed with silver, as were the edges of her skirts. Peter's inability to articulate anything intelligent might have had something to do with Diana's bare shoulders. She had lovely shoulders.

"What do you think?" Diana asked, twirling for him. Peter swallowed hard. Versace must have run out of fabric because the dress had no back.

"You look gorgeous," he managed.

Diana blushed. "Thanks."

Peter was having a hard time looking away. One thing was for sure, he would be irritated most of the evening. The moment Diana walked into that party, every man's eyes would be glued to her, and he would be jealous. And territorial. They wouldn't have any trouble getting Firat out of there, though.

"You're looking pretty spiffy yourself," Diana said with a small smile.

Judging by the heat he could feel rising in his cheeks, Peter was pretty sure he was blushing. "Thanks," he said. It came out gruff. He cleared his throat and tried again. "Thanks." That was better.

Diana stood, fidgeting, and it dawned on Peter that she

was nervous. Her body language was contained and a little awkward. Peter shook his head and smiled to himself. Hanging around her was paying off. He was nowhere near as adept at reading people as Diana, but he'd gotten quite proficient at it. Proficient enough to know he needed to put her at ease.

"Drink?"

CHAPTER THIRTEEN

"YES, PLEASE. I would."

Peter went to the bar and picked up two crystal tumblers. He poured them both a measure of the most expensive single malt on offer. Lennox was paying, after all. Peter heard a rustle of fabric behind him and looked around. Diana had moved to the window. She was looking out over the ocean, much as he'd done earlier. Peter picked up the glasses and walked over to Diana, handing her a tumbler with a flourish. "Well, my lady, I'm going to be the envy of every man at this party," he said confidently, raising his glass in a toast.

Diana laughed. It was a beautiful laugh. Husky with a crystalline edge to it. It was a type of laugh he'd never heard from her before; unabashed with an undercurrent of excitement.

"Why, thank you, kind sir. And I'm pretty sure I'll have to keep my gun handy to protect your virtue from all the women who are certain to mob you as soon as we walk in."

"I suspect a lot of the women there will be paid to do

that." They clinked glasses. "To us, and the success of our mission," Peter said.

They took a sip of their drinks. "Smooth," Diana said.

"The whisky or me?"

"The whisky." Diana's eyes crinkled in the corners as she looked at him over the rim of her glass. She took another sip. "It's pretty good. Lennox is going to have a fit when he gets the bill."

"I hardly think the price of a couple of whiskies will register. Not after getting hold of a Versace dress and a pair of strappy Louboutins."

Diana's eyes widened. She was indeed wearing Louboutins. They were white open-toed sandals, slim straps crisscrossing at her ankles. The heels were four inches high, making her nearly as tall as Peter.

Diana giggled. "You've heard of Louboutins? And know how to identify them?"

Many moons ago, Peter had had a girlfriend who'd been *obsessed* with shoes. He knew all about the signature Louboutin red sole. He decided not to share the source of his knowledge with Diana at this moment, however.

"Of course. I know lots of things you wouldn't expect a guy like me to know. That's why you love me," he said with a grin. Suddenly the atmosphere between them was charged to an almost frightening level. They both stared at each other. Diana looked stunned. Peter was unsure where to look. A jet preparing to land at Dubai International Airport roared overhead.

Diana relaxed first. She cocked her head and gave him a 1000-watt smile that pretty much floored him. "You know, I think you're right."

Peter gulped his drink and searched Diana's features, trying to figure out what she meant. The small smile that played around her lips made him think she was just kidding around. But there was a serious look in her eyes that gave him pause. Damn it! Why was it that in important moments, he lost the ability to read her?

They stared at each other for another long moment before Diana broke the spell. "Let's go," she said. She put her tumbler down on the mirrored and crystal glass table next to her with a small clink.

Peter followed suit. Diana picked up her clutch and looked at him expectantly, her eyebrows raised. He put his arm out, and she took it with a smile. "Ready, Mrs. Trevellyn?"

"Always, darling," Diana replied with a twinkle in her eye.

For the night, they were Rayne and Liam Trevellyn, an über-rich couple visiting Dubai for business and pleasure. They owned a highly successful real estate company that developed landmark building projects worldwide. Dubai was to be the site of their next development.

Diana and Peter left their suite and walked to the elevator. Peter pushed the button, and they watched the number above the doors as the lift descended from the 55th floor. "Good evening, sir, madam," the boy inside the elevator said when the doors opened.

"Evening," Peter replied smoothly.

"Hello," Diana said, with a huge smile.

"The Monarch's Suite, please," Peter said.

"Of course, sir," the young man replied. He pushed the button marked "56." Moments later, Peter and Diana stepped out into another marble foyer as opulent as the rest of the hotel. Diana's heels clicked on the floor's hard surface as they walked to the door of the suite where the party was being held. Peter casually rang the doorbell. It was time to see if the forged invitations they had would pass muster.

A large man dressed in a tuxedo answered the door. His gaze hovered over Peter and then slid to Diana. As the man took her in, a slow smile built on his lips. "My lady," he purred, completely ignoring Peter.

"Good evening," Diana replied with another huge wattage smile. Peter thrust the invitations at him. The man's gaze never wavered from Diana.

Peter gritted his teeth. "Hey you, that's my wife you're staring at," he snarled.

The guy's eyes snapped back to Peter. He swallowed hard. "My apologies, sir. Your wife is very beautiful. You are a lucky man."

"I know," Peter growled, snatching the invitations from the man's hand with a vicious swipe.

"Please, come in," the man said, standing back and quickly waving them through the door. Hallelujah, they were in.

Like the rest of the hotel, the Monarch's Suite was exquisitely ornate. This time, the marble floor comprised yellow and white tiles, while a marble staircase with an intricately designed gold balustrade unfurled in a gracious curve, leading to another floor. Women dressed in exotic gowns and dripping with jewelry accompanied men in open-necked shirts and suits, the party guests milling around, drinks in hand. Some conversed, others simply watched. It all looked quite sedate. Diana and Peter fit right in.

They were guided to the main party room by a hostess. It was set up to mimic a tent and was quite different from the open airiness of the foyer. Dark red silk accented with black velvet draped the ceiling and rear wall. White columns patterned heavily with black and gold motifs stood on either side of the steps leading to the room's entrance. Leopard-skin couches were covered in brown, beige, and orange pillows while glass and chrome tabletops supported by exuberantly designed stands that combined flourishes and curlicues in gold and black were dotted in front and to the side. Restraint had clearly not been a part of the decorator's brief.

As soon as Diana and Peter walked in and before they'd managed to get their bearings, a heavy-set, swarthy man walked up to them. He looked in his mid-twenties. Peter immediately recognized him. The man's gaze was completely focused on Diana.

"Good evening," the man said to Peter. He extended his hand, though his eyes never left Diana's cleavage. "I'm Prince Firat bin Rahid Al Omair."

"Liam Trevellyn, Your Highness." Peter shook the prince's hand firmly enough to make him wince. Shamelessly, Firat paid no heed to Peter's assertion of dominance and territory. He spoke to Diana, a predatory gleam in his eyes.

"And who might this enchanting creature be?" he asked. He had a reedy voice, pitched high for such a husky man.

Diana put her hand in his with a smile. "Rayne Trevellyn, Your Highness," she replied in a sultry tone. The prince kissed her knuckles.

"My wife," Peter added in a less friendly voice. For the second time that evening, he was ignored by a man ogling Diana.

"I'm so pleased to make your acquaintance and honored

that such a beautiful woman would grace our little soirée with her presence," Firat said to Diana.

Diana chuckled. "Why thank you, Your Highness. I'm honored to be here."

"I sincerely hope I will have the opportunity to dance later with the most beautiful jewel in the room, in fact, in all of Dubai. Of that, I am certain."

"I would enjoy that very much," Diana replied with a smile, just stopping herself from rolling her eyes.

The man was suave, Peter had to give him that. It didn't help that Diana seemed so charmed by Firat. Logically, he knew it was an act and that he had no right to be so annoyed, but logic tended to abandon him where Diana was concerned.

"And what brings you to our fair city?" the prince asked.

"Business," Peter snapped. Firat looked at him sideways as if he was of no consequence, before concentrating on Diana once more as she spoke.

"And a bit of pleasure, of course. How could we not? After all, Dubai is such a beautiful city," Diana gushed.

"You must let me show you around," Firat said. "I've lived here all my life and know every nook and cranny in our fair city. I would love to introduce you to my Dubai— the way few tourists get to experience it."

"My husband and I would love that," Diana replied. "Thank you."

Firat straightened, looking a little less pleased with his idea. "Of course. Now, if you'll excuse me, I have to greet my other guests." The prince moved off, but not before depositing another kiss on Diana's knuckles.

"The most beautiful jewel in all of Dubai," Peter mimicked. His breath left him in a whoosh when a discreet but powerful jab courtesy of Diana's elbow made contact with his gut.

"Play nice, darling," Diana said sweetly. "Remember, we'll need the prince's *cooperation* if our *deal* is to go through."

Peter groaned. She was right. They had to play their parts.

"Drink?" he asked.

"Yes, please. Orange juice. I need to be on my game."

"Looks like that's all they're serving."

Peter made his way over to the bar. He looked around the room while he waited for the barman's attention. The party was rather quiet, still. Staid, even. Peter walked back to Diana and handed her a crystal glass filled with orange juice. "It's a bit quiet, this party."

"Mmm," Diana replied.

"Lennox implied it would be wilder. We'll have difficulty extracting Firat without anyone noticing if the pace doesn't pick up a bit."

Peter noticed Diana's eyes roaming over the room. Her jaw tightened. "What's up?"

"I'm wondering what the game is here. It all feels so *fake*."

Peter straightened his shoulders. "Well, shall we mingle and see what we can find out?"

"Good idea." They moved off to circulate, talking to partygoers, most of them business people, some royalty, while keeping their eye on Firat the entire time.

CHAPTER FOURTEEN

"**G**OT ANYTHING USEFUL?" They had been schmoozing non-stop for two hours when Diana pulled Peter to one side.

"Firat is the youngest son of Dubai's ruler, which means he's unlikely to ever ascend the throne. He has two older brothers so he's rich and aimless. Add some testosterone and resentment to that mix, and he's a ripe and valuable target for recruitment to a terrorist organization, no question," Peter said.

"What could his goal be, I wonder?" Diana replied.

"Perhaps joining ILIF has something to do with removing his competition so he can ascend to Dubai's throne instead of his brothers? Fratricide, even patricide, isn't uncommon here, so the idea isn't out of the question."

"It would make him a psychopath."

"Yeah, tell me something I don't know. Can't say I fell in love with him based on his earlier performance. Did you?"

"Not exactly," Diana replied.

"So what did you find out?"

"Firat's father, Sheikh Rahid bin Said Al Omair is a

popular ruler and quite progressive, at least by comparison to his counterparts. He's responsible for much of Dubai's development, which gives the country its position and power in the region. It used to rely on oil production for most of its revenue, but the sheikh saw the risks of relying solely on that and encouraged diversification into tourism, banking, and technology. The increase in revenues has meant that the people of Dubai haven't suffered during the various crises that have severely impacted the price of oil and affected other countries in the region. It has one of the fastest growing economies, even though oil production is a mere five percent of the emirate's revenues."

Peter looked at Diana dubiously. "That's quite a lecture."

"I was cornered by an economics professor from one of the American university campuses they have out here," Diana said. "The sheikh, Firat's father, is well thought of here, but there is one issue. There are rumors that he's considering giving women more rights. That's displeasing the old guard, including other leaders in the country who are claiming it would set an unfortunate precedent. So there is some domestic political turmoil." Diana looked from side to side at the scene around her, her earrings jangling. "Could it be, as you said, that Firat's connection to ILIF is part of a bigger plan to overthrow his father?"

"But why would he do that? For what reason? Money? Wealth? Surely he has enough of that?"

"Power for its own sake? They have egos the size of continents, these people." Diana fingered one of her diamond earrings. They were so long, they were pulling at her ears.

"Or it's something else. Perhaps he objects to his father's policies. Perhaps they are at odds ideologically."

"I think any of those motivations are possible, although ideology doesn't seem to be his strong point beyond the worship of the almighty dollar. Maybe he really is as childish as he seems and is lashing out at his father in any way he can. Perhaps Firat wants to use his terrorist connections to embarrass the sheikh, and it's no more complicated than that. An act of rebellion."

The party was still deathly quiet. Diana turned to face Peter and whispered in his ear. "So, what do you think? Time to come up with a 'Plan B'?"

Peter sighed and glanced around. Everything was just as calm and low-key as it had been earlier. People were simply chatting and networking. Over the hum of conversation, he heard the occasional peal of laughter, and glasses clinking. But wild, it was not. He could even hear the muzak over the gentle hubbub. "I guess so," Peter murmured, glancing around uneasily.

Diana put her glass down and prepared to slip away when a loud gong sounded. "Game time?" Peter said, his voice low. Firat's large bulk walked into the middle of the room, his arms outspread.

"Ladies and gentlemen, now that everyone has finally arrived, let the entertainment commence!" He rubbed his hands vigorously and clapped twice.

Diana blinked as the lights dimmed, the music segued to something more upbeat, and small white lights started to float around the room in a circular motion. Bottles were switched on the wait staff's trays, replacing the sparkling water and fruit juices of earlier with all manner of wine and spirits. As the alcohol flowed, women dressed in brightly colored bikinis and feathers streamed into the room and quickly draped themselves all over the men, even the ones whose wives were present.

Peter shook his head. "Well, I guess it's back to 'Plan A.'"

Diana nodded. "Thankfully. I was not looking forward to propositioning His Highness's assness."

Peter laughed. "Is that what you were thinking?" He grinned at her. "Now I'm really glad we can stick with our plan." He looked around the room, "So, how long do you think it'll take them to get plastered?"

Diana tapped a finger against her lips as she surveyed the room, which was now a hedonic paradise. "I'm thinking about an hour."

Peter cocked an eyebrow. "You don't drink much, do you? I'm pretty sure in about half that time, most of these people won't remember their own names, let alone the people they're hanging off."

Peter was right. Thirty minutes later, everyone was either drunk or well on the way. "For a country where alcohol is not easily accessible, they sure can put it away," Diana murmured.

"It's *because* it's not freely available. Like kids let out of school for the summer, they make the most of it when they can. Not that I know anything about that," Peter added putting his palms up. Diana regarded him skeptically.

Peter glanced around. The partygoers were off the leash, guzzling down everything from whisky to wine like it was water. "Just goes to show how making something illegal doesn't always achieve the desired results."

"Is that an indication of your broader political values?" Diana teased.

"Might be."

Diana smiled. Peter might come across as a bluff grunt at times, but she knew that at heart, he thought and cared deeply about issues that affected people, especially those he was close to. Before she had a chance to say more, Peter saw Firat heading toward them. He nodded in Firat's direction. Diana looked over.

"Showtime," she whispered under her breath. She fidgeted with her clutch, palming something in her hand. Peter knew it was the vial of scopolamine that Lennox had procured for them and that they would use on Firat.

"I don't love the idea of scopolamine, you know. We went to such trouble to keep it off the streets of Vancouver and now here we are, using it on someone," Peter murmured in Diana's ear.

"Needs must, darling. We're not going to hurt him, or even rob him. And we don't have much time. We need to get him talking."

Firat walked shakily over to them, and in the way of young bucks used to having anything and anyone they wanted, he grabbed Diana by the wrist and hauled her off to the bar. Peter bristled but quietly followed them at an appreciable distance so that Firat wouldn't notice. The prince leaned on the bar talking animatedly to Diana. Peter watched her closely. Only he saw her swipe her palm over Firat's drink. Delivery was complete. Now, they just had to wait.

CHAPTER FIFTEEN

H ALF AN HOUR later, Diana and Peter
stumbled into their suite with a sagging but very
amenable Firat. "We need to talk," Diana whispered to Peter.

Peter hauled Firat off to the bedroom. "Wait here," he
said to the lump flailing around on the bed Peter had so
coveted earlier.

Firat grinned up at him like a lunatic. "Of course," he
replied.

Peter left the room and locked the door behind him.
"What's up?" he said to Diana.

"That idiot in there will never make a good asset.
Lennox would be wasting his time." Diana rubbed the
bridge of her nose. "Besides the fact that his only convic-
tions lie at the bottom of a bottle and his only goal is to get
into the pants of as many women as possible, his values are
so warped that he'll do anything to spite his old man. He is
way too unstable, self-obsessed, and egotistical to trust even
mildly. He's liable to turn us in to his ILIF friends the

moment we release him. We could never trust him or even manipulate him more than once."

"You managed to figure all this out on the way up here?"

"More or less. The alcohol and the scopolamine did their job, and a quick chat at the bar before we brought him up here told me all I needed to know. Yuck. I wish I could wipe my memory of the disgusting suggestions and anti-daddy rants he kept spewing. He's beyond selfish, and well, let's just say he's one of the few people that might make me rethink my stance on torture." Peter gave a lop-sided smile.

Diana continued. "The risk is just too great. He's such a blundering idiot, he'd end up giving the game away. He couldn't fool anyone. He may be brilliant in the boardroom, but anything beyond that and he's a complete, total, and utter mess. And way too compromised by his base values."

"Well, then, I guess we stick to the plan. We get the intel we need and disappoint Lennox. I can't say that I'm unhappy we don't have to deal with Firat any longer than necessary. And the scopolamine was a good call."

"We'll take him back to the party after we're done, hang around for a little while, and then disappear. Tomorrow, he won't remember a thing."

"Sounds good. Shall we?" Peter nodded toward the bedroom door. "The sooner we get rid of him, the better."

"Let's go. I'll start by setting out the rules; that he needs to respond to our directions," Diana said.

"Is that necessary? Won't he do our bidding because of the scopolamine?"

"I want to reinforce the idea that he needs to cooperate."

Peter unlocked the bedroom door and walked into the room. He stopped in his tracks. Firat was lying flat on his back, eyes closed with both his hands on the pillow, his curled fists laying on either side of his ears. He looked like a massive, grotesque baby.

"Oh no," groaned Peter. "Please tell me you're not asleep."

"I'm not asleep," Firat said obediently as he sat up.

Peter breathed a sigh of relief. "Follow me," he said curtly. Firat stood and followed Peter into the suite's living room like a well-trained puppy.

"Sit down." Firat sat.

"Now, you will answer all our questions truthfully and give us all the information we need," Diana said. She stood over him. Peter pulled up a chair and sat directly opposite Firat.

"What do you know about the assassination attempt on Senator Riley Greene?" Peter asked Firat.

Firat looked at them blankly. "Firat!" Diana snapped. The man jumped.

"Yes?" he asked, mildly. Peter repeated the question.

"I don't know anything," Firat said. Peter opened his mouth to argue.

Diana raised her hand to stop him. "Why did ILIF try to kill a Canadian senator?"

"Because he was threatening to back out of the deal. I gave the order!" Firat said triumphantly before he sobered with the effort and slumped in his seat.

"He obviously likes you more than me," Peter said.

Diana shook her head. "It's not that. He probably doesn't know the senator's name. Scopolamine makes people very literal."

But Firat hadn't finished. "The Canadian senator had our guy killed, but he paid up, so the deal's back on."

Diana turned back to Firat. "What deal do you have with the Canadian senator?"

"He's going to pay us to take the responsibility for the bombing in Canada."

Peter and Diana exchanged glances. "What bombing?" Peter asked.

"What, what?" Firat hiccupped.

Peter inhaled and spoke sharply. "What bombing is ILIF supposed to take responsibility for?" he said as though speaking to a child.

"The one the Canadian senator is organizing, of course." Firat was slurring his words and finished his sentence with a giggle.

"Why would he do that?"

"Why would who do what?" Firat asked.

"Why would the Canadian senator pay ILIF to take responsibility for a bombing?"

"He wants to become Prime Minister, silly," Firat replied.

"Tell us what you know about this bombing," Diana said.

"It's scheduled to take place soon. In one of Canada's major cities."

"Which city is the bombing planned for?"

Firat shrugged. "We don't know the details, they haven't told us. We'll know when it happens, it'll be obvious. We'll release a statement."

"How much was the Canadian senator going to pay you?" Peter asked.

"Twenty million dollars," Firat replied. "Half now, half after the job was done."

Peter whistled. "That's a lot of money."

"Not so much," Firat replied. "I paid that for a racehorse for my birthday."

Diana turned to Peter and nodded toward the bedroom. They left Firat sitting in his chair and walked into the next room. Peter kept the door open and his eye on the prisoner.

"Why would Greene bomb his own people? Why would he think that would help him become Prime Minister?" Diana said quietly.

Peter shook his head. "Because he's insane?"

"I think that goes without saying. But he obviously thinks it will benefit him in some way. But how?"

Peter pondered the situation. "What's the first thing that happened after 9/11?"

"Tighter security," Diana said.

"Yes, but what else? What else happened that, if it happened again, would benefit a politician like Greene?"

Diana considered for a moment. "Public opinion changed."

"Exactly," Peter said. "Politicians who'd been advocating for peace and withdrawal from the Middle East fell out of favor. People wanted revenge. Attack someone in their home country, threaten their safety and their ongoing sense of security, and they suddenly become a lot less forgiving and pacifistic."

"And since our current PM wants to pull our troops out of Afghanistan, he'll lose favor with the people if there's a similar event. They'll turn to someone like Greene, who's advocating for greater intervention, war in fact," Diana said, finishing Peter's thought.

"It's the only thing that makes sense," Peter added.

Diana snorted. "That *is* insane."

"Building power by killing innocent people and entering into a war is the oldest game in the book," Peter reminded her.

CHAPTER SIXTEEN

"WHO WOULD BANKROLL Greene to pull off something like this? Who would want someone like him in Canada's top job?" Peter said.

"Kloch?"

"He can't be his only partner. Kloch may have money but twenty million dollars? He has nowhere near that amount. He is entirely too small. Someone else is involved— someone with a lot of money and a lot of clout. And there's the other point to consider: ILIF hired Garibaldi to terminate Greene because he was going to back out of the deal. Why would he want to back out?"

"Perhaps he got cold feet?"

"Someone capable of planning to kill his own countrymen to become Prime Minister is unlikely to get cold feet," Peter replied. He looked at Firat. "Let's ask him."

Diana walked over to where Firat was waiting patiently. "Why did the Canadian senator try to back out of the deal?"

"Because we demanded he arrange for two assassinations on Canadian soil. He didn't want to do it," Firat said slowly.

"Who did you want assassinated?"

"My father and older brother."

"Your father? Sheikh Rahid bin Said Al Omair? He's the target of a planned assassination?"

"Yes. And the Crown Prince," Firat said, a smug smile settling sleepily on his face.

"Why were your father and brother targets?" Diana asked.

"So I can become the puppet master," Firat replied.

Peter was ready for him. "There's still another person between you and the throne. Your other brother," he pointed out.

"Yes," Firat replied with a grin.

"Where was this going to happen?" Peter asked.

"The Vancouver Opera."

"Why the opera?"

"Because my father and my older brother, the Crown Prince will be attending a performance of Madame Butterfly along with my sister."

"God, this is turning into such a mess," Diana whispered. She turned back to Firat. "So, why didn't the Canadian senator want to assassinate your father and brother?" It seemed a ridiculous question but the entire scenario was outlandish.

"Because ILIF refuses to take responsibility for their deaths. We want the senator to find a Canadian national to do that," Firat replied. "My father is a beloved figure in Dubai. If the people think the sheikh was killed by ILIF, it will cause my father's people to turn against us. If they think he was killed by a Canadian, or even better the Canadian government, they will turn in favor *of* us." He lifted his fingers in air quotes. "'Our' subsequent bombing of a Canadian target will be justified in the eyes of Dubai's people. ILIF will become a powerful force in Dubai. We will have the whole country behind us, public opinion in Canada will support military intervention in the Middle East, the Canadian senator will become Prime Minister, and my brother will ascend to the throne. See? How many birds is that with one stone? Three? Four? Five? Isn't it a beautiful plan?"

"Why the hell do you want that? You'd have the might of Western military forces bombing you to high heaven. The whole of the Middle East will be in uproar!" Peter exclaimed.

"I know. Isn't it great? And my brother will be in charge of the whole pickle!" Firat giggled again before settling down.

"And where will you be while all this carnage is taking place?"

Firat shrugged. "Miles away. London, Paris, New York, the Med. As far away from Dubai as it is possible to get. I went to Harvard, you know. I have friends all over."

"So you're working for ILIF, stiffing them at the same time by pretending to believe in their ideals, killing your father and brother, starting a war, and leaving another brother in charge of sorting out crazy town?"

"Ye-hes," Firat said in a sing-song voice.

Peter looked at Diana. "I told you he's a lot smarter than Lennox gave him credit for."

Diana exhaled through her nose. "So is the deal to kill your father still on?"

"Yes."

"When is your father's visit scheduled?

"He leaves Dubai the day after tomorrow."

"Do you know who's to carry out the bombing?"

"Nope, that's all done by them over there."

"The people who are paying you to take responsibility, yes?" Peter confirmed.

"Yep. The senator's people."

"Is Bernard Kloch involved?"

"Who?"

"Have you heard of Blue Panther?"

"No."

"When is this bombing supposed to take place?"

"I don't know."

"What is the target for the bombing?"

"I told you, I don't know." Peter looked at the ceiling, his hands on his hips. He blew out his cheeks.

"If you were going to make twenty million dollars from the deal with the Canadian senator, why plan to kill him?" Firat shrugged.

"All stupid ILIF is interested in is giving their cause legitimacy, but it's much more important to me to have my father and brother killed than earn a few measly million dollars. We'd have found another Western fool to go along with our plan. There are plenty of them around. People who want to start wars, profit from them, gain power." He giggled. He started to slump sideways on the bed.

"Write down the bank and the account to which the money was wired," Diana ordered him. Firat dutifully wrote the details down.

Diana turned to Peter. "Let's get him back. Lennox can decide what to do with him from here. We've got to get this sorted out."

Peter yanked Firat up. "Hey, man," Firat protested weakly.

"Shut up. We're taking you back to the party now. Act happy, okay?"

"But aren't I staying here with you? With *her*?" Firat lunged out and started fumbling with Diana's dress. Peter grabbed his wrists. As he pushed Firat out of the room, Diana saw Peter clip Firat hard in the chest with his elbow. Later he would claim it was an accident.

"I can't believe Greene is this insane," Lennox said back at TFI headquarters. "What has this world come to when our politicians are willing to sacrifice their own people for personal gain?"

After dispatching Firat back to the party, Diana and Peter checked out of their hotel and dashed back to Kandahar for a rapid-fire debrief with Lennox.

Peter snorted. "Have you ever heard of a politician *not* interested in personal gain?"

Lennox shook his head. "No, but neither have I heard of one willing to go to these extremes." Lennox sighed. "Too bad you couldn't turn Firat. He would have been a great resource."

Diana shrugged. "Trust me, he would have ended up ruining everything. You can still get intel from him. Just send someone in with some scopolamine. Problem solved."

"We'll see," Lennox said. "In the meantime, good luck. You know our Canadian office will help in any way they can. We'll keep our ears to the ground to see if we can come up with anything more."

Diana nodded. "Thanks." She didn't smile at him. She couldn't.

Lennox hesitated. He leaned in. "Diana, I'm sorry—"

"Forget it. Water under the bridge." Diana would put

their conflict behind her, but she would never trust Ethan Lennox again.

"It's been good to see you, Lennox," Peter said, his tone belying his words. He, too, was glad to leave what now felt like the oppressive atmosphere of TFI.

"You know the offer still stands. You're wasted at VPD. There's always a place for you here."

"Thanks." Peter shook Lennox's hand. "I'll keep that in mind."

CHAPTER SEVENTEEN

PETER AND DIANA arrived back in Vancouver in the late afternoon sunshine and went straight to CSIS headquarters. When they arrived, they were quickly ushered into a conference room where Amanda Stone, Clive Inglewood, and Bill Donaldson were waiting for them, as well as two men from the Royal Canadian Mounted Police's counter-terrorism unit. The atmosphere was electric.

There was absolutely no cordiality. Peter and Diana had barely entered the room before the assembled group assaulted them with questions. Diana raised a hand. Everyone quieted.

"I understand the urgency, but if we all talk at once, we won't get anything done. First of all, let's get the introductions out of the way," Diana said, turning to the two Mounties. "I'm Diana Hunter, and this is my partner, Detective Peter Hopkinson."

"I'm Sergeant Major Owen Lyndon, and this is Staff Sergeant Major Christian Burke. Good to meet you, ma'am, detective," one of the Mounties said. The other merely nodded. Both men were high-ranking officers. They were taut, fit, military-type men with sharp haircuts. Lyndon looked to be in his mid-forties. He was rugged and sported a generous mustache. Burke, slightly younger, was fresh-faced and boyish-looking.

"Likewise," Diana said. "Now, how about you listen while we tell you everything we know, and then we can formulate a plan of action?"

Peter and Diana provided all the salient points they had gleaned during their mission, minus any details concerning TFI's base, which were classified on a need-to-know basis. No one at the meeting needed to know.

Once they had finished, the mood in the room was grim. Before Diana's and Peter's arrival, Lennox had given Amanda, Donaldson, and the Mounties a phone briefing, but he hadn't told them everything. He hadn't told them that one of their own senators was behind this planned atrocity. It was tough to contemplate.

"Can't we just arrest Greene as a threat to national security?" Diana asked.

Sergeant Major Owen Lyndon concurred. "I agree. We have to pick him up. Drill him."

Donaldson and Stone both shook their heads. "We have no evidence. We can't just pick him up off the street. He's a public figure. He has powerful friends who will shut us down," Donaldson said. "Let's be smart about this."

"RCMP can deal with him, squeeze him. We can't pussyfoot around on this. The risk is too great. We need to pull him in and get him talking. We could have a bloodbath on our hands otherwise. If we don't know when or where it is, how will we stop it? Who wants to explain we couldn't upset a few egos when we're knee-deep in bodies after a mass casualty incident?"

"We have to follow the rule of law. Until we have some hard proof of his involvement, everything is just conjecture. This Firat person could be winding us up," Amanda said.

"That's simply ridiculous. If your intel is credible, we have plenty of grounds to interview him. Leave him to us. RCMP is experienced in this kind of thing. We'll soon get the intel we need."

"We have no grounds, Lyndon," Amanda repeated.

"Greene is more useful left out in the field being watched, anyway," Peter asserted.

"Peter's right. We need to find out who his cohorts are. Who would want their man on the Canadian hot seat?" Diana offered.

"Greene may be merely the last link in the chain. There must be others who are backing him. Bigger, more influential people," Amanda concurred. "We have to find the rot and remove it completely or it will be the equivalent of putting a band-aid on a gunshot wound."

"But we risk a terrorist incident!" Burke exclaimed. It was an unavoidable truth, and it brought the conversation to a halt. Every person in the room nodded or muttered their agreement.

Donaldson broke the silence. "Our hands are tied. Did this Firat person say anything about who's doing the groundwork?"

Peter shook his head. "He said he didn't know."

"Was he telling the truth?" Sergeant Major Lyndon asked.

"The veracity of his statements is the one thing we are certain of," Diana said. "Whether the information he gave is accurate or not, we can't be sure, but he was telling us the truth as he knows it."

"How can you be so certain?" Staff Sergeant Major Burke said.

Peter turned to him. "Let's just say we can, okay, and leave it at that," he said, his jaw tight. He and Diana were under no obligation to any of the agencies present. CSIS would not have any issue with intel extracted with the use of a drug, and Peter was sure Donaldson wouldn't bat an eyelash. But he didn't know the RCMP men, and he didn't want to risk them discounting the intel because of the way it had been obtained. The threat was credible. That was all they needed to know.

"I don't know," Burke said, looking skeptical. "It's CSIS's job to warn us of impending terror attacks, but our job to avert them."

Amanda cocked an eyebrow. "And I believe that's exactly what's happening here. We're warning you of an impending major attack, yet you'd rather argue over the legitimacy of the details."

"But you're not giving us the tools that will allow us to do our job. We need to interrogate Greene. Screw the law. The danger to the public is too great," Burke retorted.

Amanda was Burke's senior by a significant amount, but he was unfazed. He opened his mouth to say something more, but Lyndon cut him off.

"We need to urgently confirm the target of this proposed bomb attack. We need to move to a code red in all major cities and intercept chatter on the ground to uncover what's going on. The plans may be well underway and the bombers in situ. They could be somewhere on our streets as we speak." When he saw Amanda was about to say something, Lyndon continued quickly. "Don't you agree, Diana?"

"It's very possible. What do we have coming up?" Diana replied.

"We have the marathon, the Opera Festival, the Jazz Festival next month, and the Celebration of Light after that. And that's just Vancouver. We need to narrow down the possibilities," Donaldson said.

Clive Inglewood spoke up, making everyone start. "I say we follow the money."

"Excuse me?" Lyndon said.

"We follow the money. Greene is involved in this big time. And we know that Bernard Kloch is a big ally of Greene's. He might be covering for Greene or enabling him. We don't have evidence to squeeze the information out of either of them, so we follow the money. We know a payment of ten million was made and another ten—"

"Do you think that there's only been one payment of ten million dollars made in the entire world in the last what, shall we say, six months?" Lyndon snapped. Diana thought he was being unnecessarily aggressive now.

"It's very likely that it wouldn't be paid in one lump sum either. They probably paid multiple amounts, using multiple banks, accounts, and dates. The trail will be long and complicated," Diana added evenly.

Clive looked so dejected that Diana felt sorry for him despite their past. "But that's no reason not to chase it. We did get the details of the account that the ten million was transferred into. You could work backward from there," Diana said.

Clive sat up in his chair. He licked his lips. "If you can give me that information, I'll get our people on it. Shouldn't take too long."

"How soon?" Lyndon asked.

"Depends on where the bank is," Clive replied.

"The British Virgin Islands," Peter said.

"Then I should be able to get you the first pass information in twenty-four hours," Clive said confidently.

Lyndon gave him a skeptical look. "We are the Canadian Security and Intelligence Service, you know," Clive responded.

Amanda backed him up. "We know how to get intelligence *quickly*."

"If we can make a connection to Greene, we can bring him in. The Deputy Commissioner will fold if we have evidence. I'll personally lean on him. I'd be happy to," Donaldson said. "I'll get a judge on standby to give us a warrant for his arrest."

"If we can prove Greene is associating with terrorists, we don't need a warrant. We can pick him up on the grounds of being a threat to national security," Lyndon said.

"You might be able to do that, but VPD certainly can't," Donaldson said.

"Then we'll pick him up ourselves."

"Fine, but I want Diana and Hopkinson along with you. This has been their case from the start."

Lyndon had the grace to agree this time and dipped his head minutely. "Of course. I wouldn't have it any other way."

"What about the sheikh?" Peter said before anyone moved. "We have to warn him and also prepare for an alternative strike."

"Good point. Okay, people, let's get to work. I'll get in touch with the UAE Embassy and get the sheikh's itinerary," Amanda said. "RCMP and CSIS will start working our networks. We'll lean on them, hard if necessary, and put everyone on high alert. We'll draw up a list of all the high-profile events we have coming up and liaise with the RCMP about stepping up security for them.

"But uncovering the target has to be the top priority. We don't want to get caught with our pants down while we're looking the wrong way," Amanda concluded, mixing her metaphors but getting her point across. "Clive, chase the money angle. Donaldson, get that judge on standby just in case. Code red everyone, we have a crisis on our hands. We may not have long, and those cells may well be in place by now. We have to find them before we have a bloodbath on our hands." This was Amanda at her best—authoritative, competent, and incisive. Everyone nodded in agreement.

"You and Diana head home and get some rest," Donaldson said to Peter. "We'll call you as soon as we have more information."

Diana didn't want to leave. She was reluctant to cede control. Something might go terribly wrong. But logically, there wasn't much for her to do until more information came to light.

"Need a lift?" Peter whispered. Diana gave a slight, reluctant nod.

"Diana and I will head out, then," Peter announced to the room.

"We'll call you as soon as there's news," Amanda promised.

CHAPTER EIGHTEEN

THE FOLLOWING DAY, Diana hadn't been in her office for fifteen minutes when her cell phone rang.

"Diana, it's Amanda. I forwarded Sheikh Al Omair's itinerary to you and VPD. I also got the sheikh's people to agree to a meeting. He's expecting you at noon."

"Noon? Where?" Diana asked.

"He's staying at the Fairmont."

"Thanks, Amanda. I'll call Peter, and we'll head on over."

"I suppose I don't need to—"

"Remind me to be diplomatic?" Diana said with a chuckle. "Don't worry, I'll be gentle when I tell him his son is trying to kill him."

"He might not believe you. Be clear and direct," Amanda said.

"I know, I know."

"Give me an update when you're done." The words sounded like an order, but Amanda's tone was soft enough not to raise Diana's hackles.

"I'll call as soon as we're finished. Any news from Clive about the money?"

"Nothing so far, but he should have something by early this afternoon."

"I wish we could pick Greene up. Throw him in a cell for a few hours and let him stew. Maybe he'd come to his senses and start talking," Diana said, massaging her neck muscles with her free hand as she spoke.

"Me too, but you know we don't have the power to do that, and the VPD won't do it without a warrant."

"I know. But still, I wish we could."

"You and me both," Amanda replied.

"I'll get in touch later."

"Great. Thanks, Diana. It's good to be working with you again. I've missed you."

Forty-five minutes later, Peter and Diana stood in front of the door to the Fairmont's Royal Suite, showing the two bodyguards their credentials.

"You may go in," one of the men said in strongly accented English.

The two of them stepped through the door, walking into an ostentatious room with a fireplace, couch, and chairs at one end and a dining table at the other. The cream and pale yellow décor beautifully offset the mahogany furniture. Everything from the light fixtures to the art on the wall was expensive and elegant and created an atmosphere of luxury and warmth for someone with discerning tastes and deep pockets.

An internal door opened, and a short, trim man in his early thirties, dressed in a sharply tailored suit, came out to greet them. "Hello, my name is Halil, and I'm His Highness Sheikh Rahid bin Said Al Omair's secretary. I'm also his eldest son," he said, shaking Peter's hand. To her surprise, he also shook Diana's.

"I'm Detective Peter Hopkinson, and this is my partner, Diana Hunter," Peter said.

A voice boomed from across the room. "Halil, don't keep the police officers! Bring them to me."

Diana shifted her gaze and saw a man in his late fifties standing by the dining table. He was fit and trim, and she had to admit, extremely attractive with silver hair and a closely cropped mustache and goatee. What surprised her more was that he wore a dark gray suit rather than the traditional Arabic *keffiyeh*, and *dishdash*.

"Of course, Your Highness," Halil said quickly, though the half-smile he wore indicated he was used to his father's impatience. "Please, come," he said to Peter and Diana.

"This is Detective Peter Hopkinson and his partner, Diana Hunter, from the Vancouver Police Department, Your Highness," Halil said with a short bow.

"Yes, Halil, I heard," the sheikh said.

"*As salaam alaikum*, Your Highness," Diana said, fluently.

"*Wa alaikum salaam*, Ms. Hunter," the sheikh replied. He grasped her hand, his eye contact strong. She noticed approval in his eyes.

The sheikh shook Peter's hand and invited them to sit at the table. Peter pulled out the chair next to the sheikh for Diana to sit on. Her heart flooded with appreciation at the gesture. Once everyone was seated, they waited for the sheikh to begin the conversation.

"So, what can I do for the Vancouver Police Department?"

"We are here on behalf of several organizations, including the Canadian Security and Intelligence Service, Your Highness. Not just VPD," Diana said. The sheikh's eyebrows rose, but he said nothing. "Unfortunately, we have credible intelligence that your life is in danger. An attack is to take place while you are in Vancouver." Diana watched the sheikh closely for his reaction.

"What?" Halil exclaimed. "How can this be?" Halil's jaw dropped and his eyebrows rose. Pink spots appeared on his cheeks, and his eyes were hard and flinty. Halil was genuinely surprised, unlike his father.

The sheikh's look of astonishment lasted too long to be real. His expression was asymmetrical, and the left side of his face displayed a greater level of intensity. True emotions show symmetrically on the face, both sides being similarly intense. Al Omair was unsurprised that someone was trying to kill him.

"Halil, let them speak," the sheikh said, lifting his hand to silence his son.

"My partner and I personally collected the intelligence from our source in Dubai. According to the source, the attack will take place at the Vancouver Opera."

The sheikh pursed his lips and turned them down, nodding his head several times in quick succession. "Really? Not many people know of my plan to attend the opera tonight. Very few people are aware of this trip at all. This is a private visit. I'm here to see my daughter, and only those closest to me know my itinerary."

"Right now, it doesn't matter how the information leaked, Your Highness. What's important is that we protect you," Peter said. "We'd like to assign you additional security detail."

"But if you are aware of when the attack is to take place,

why would you need to do that? Can you not just secure the opera house?" It was clear from his body language that the sheikh didn't want them anywhere near him. He had crossed his legs, leaned back in his chair, and crossed his arms at the wrists.

"We can protect you, Your Highness," Diana said, her tone soft. "There's no guarantee your enemies will not change their plans. You are the target, not the opera. There are other elements at play, and they could get to you. And that's why we'd prefer you had additional security with you at all times."

The sheikh's expression was inscrutable. Diana licked her lips and took a deep breath. They needed more to convince Al Omair that the threat to his life was real. Diana glanced over at Peter nervously.

"There's no delicate way of putting this, Your Highness," Peter said. "Your son, Firat, is a member of the group arranging your assassination. He's been heavily involved in the planning."

CHAPTER NINETEEN

"**T**HIS IS NOT possible!" Al Omair exclaimed, leaning forward and banging the table with the palm of his hand. The higher pitch of his voice, the faster cadence of his speech, and his chin thrust forward were all signs of anger. Diana would have assumed it was aimed at her had the sheikh not broken eye contact and looked to his left. He was recalling something. A memory had sparked his anger. And then, his eyes dulled. He was resigned to something.

"You are not as surprised as you want us to believe, Your Highness," Diana said softly.

The sheikh's eyes cut back to her. "Are you accusing me of lying?" he snapped.

"No, but I do believe you are trying to protect Firat."

"I cannot believe my son would have me killed," the sheikh said slowly. He crossed his arms and leaned back—another distancing tactic, and one that said he didn't believe a word he was saying. Coupled with the avoidance of his son's name, it was obvious to Diana that the sheikh not only knew his son was trying to kill him but was expecting it.

"Has he tried to have you killed before?" Diana said.

"Of course not!" the sheikh exclaimed.

"Your words say one thing, but your body language tells me something else." Diana was taking a big risk. She, a woman, was challenging a sheikh. Diana was stepping over some big, time-honored boundaries. As she spoke, Al Omair cradled one hand in the other. "You were nodding just now. The real answer to my question was 'yes,' wasn't it? You've been caressing one hand with the other, a self-comforting gesture. That, and your one-sided shrug are things people do when they don't believe what they're saying. Your Highness, I believe you're protecting your son, and unfortunately, in doing so, you're risking the lives of your other children, your personal security detail, and the members of the public who will be in your vicinity."

The sheikh looked at her. "I was told you are very astute, Ms. Hunter. I can see why." Diana's lips parted slightly, and her breathing quickened. The sheikh smiled. "Canada is not the only country with an intelligence service, you know."

"Of course, Your Highness. It's just that I'm surprised I'm considered important enough to be brought to your attention."

"Your background makes for interesting reading, Ms. Hunter, currently of VPD, TFI, formerly of CSIS." The sheikh looked at Peter. "As does yours, Major."

Peter shifted in his seat uncomfortably. Diana acknowledged the sheikh's words with a small smile. He sat up straighter, his voice stern now. "My son has tried to have me eliminated before, which is why he is watched closely. I know about your visit to my country."

"Why haven't you done anything?" Peter asked.

"What would you have me do? Have him executed?" the sheikh snapped.

"Some time in prison might give him the opportunity to think about things," Peter responded.

"You are correct. Unfortunately though, while I have considered this course of action, there has been insufficient physical evidence to convict him. He's a smart boy, always has been. He tends to behave to excess but is clever enough to rein himself in just enough to be effective. At least, thus far. Things will catch up with him, eventually. They always do." The sheikh bowed his head and looked down as his hand touched his forehead. It was an indication of deep shame.

"Do you really not have the evidence?" Diana asked. The sheikh looked up quickly, surprise on his face. It was real surprise this time.

"Of course not," he said. And he was telling the truth. "If I did, I would take action."

The sheikh's features hardened once more. "I love all my children dearly, but ambition, ego, and resentment blind Firat. I cannot sacrifice myself or my other children, but I need to have evidence of his misbehavior."

"Your Highness," Diana said, "all we want to do is protect you. We want to ensure you enjoy your time in our country and leave here safe and sound. We have intelligence that clearly states that a threat to your life has been planned while you are with us. I'm sure your men are well-trained, but we insist that you allow us to assign additional protection to you. We also ask that you avoid the Vancouver Opera and other major public situations for the duration of your trip."

The sheikh studied Diana and Peter silently for a few moments. "I'm sorry, but I cannot accept your offer."

"But, Your Highness—" Peter said.

The sheikh held up a hand. "If I were to accept protection from your country, if it got out that my life was threatened by my own son, what message would that send my people? I would be humiliated. No. I cannot accept. I thank you for the offer, and I will change my public plans. I will not go to the opera tonight, but I cannot accept your protection. I will make my own arrangements."

Peter opened his mouth to say something, but Diana gently placed a hand on his arm. "Your decision is disappointing but very well, Your Highness. If you become party to more information or something happens that concerns you, please call us." Diana took out her business card and pushed it toward Halil.

"Certainly, Ms. Hunter. Once again, thank you for coming." Halil was remarkably calm, considering they had just told him that his life was in danger. The sheikh crossed his arms and leaned back once more. He had dismissed them. Diana and Peter said their goodbyes and left. Peter was visibly rattled but restrained himself until they were outside.

"What the hell, Diana? His son wants to blow him up and not for the first time, and he *still* doesn't want protection?"

Diana shrugged. "It's all about politics and image. He has to show strength, and in his eyes, accepting our protection makes him look weak."

"I know, but he'd rather be dead, his children too? Not to mention the innocents around him that could get caught up in his mess!"

"I know it's frustrating, but it is what it is. We can't force him to accept protection. We can put a detail on him and they'll keep an eye on him from a distance."

Diana pulled out her phone. "I have to call Amanda. Hopefully, Clive has something for us."

Just then, Peter's phone vibrated. "Hey, what's up?" he said into it. Diana waited silently. "We'll be right there," he added, frowning.

"What's wrong?" Diana asked when he ended the call.

"Clive couldn't find a concrete link between Greene and the money, but the RCMP barged in and arrested him, anyway. Said they didn't need a warrant because of suspected terrorist activities, blah, blah. He's in lockup at VPD right now."

"Okay, so what's the problem? We knew they were hotheaded, and Greene is in it up to his neck. It doesn't seem like the worst decision ever made."

"That idiot Lyndon refused to wait for us."

"And . . . ?

"Greene demanded his lawyer who is now screaming bloody murder. We're never going to get anything out of him now."

Diana narrowed her eyes. "Oh, don't be so certain. Let's get down there before the lawyer forces VPD to release him."

CHAPTER TWENTY

"**D**AMN YOU, RCMP," Donaldson said. "You jumped the gun, as usual. I told you to wait for evidence, for Diana, but you wouldn't listen." Diana was standing outside the interrogation room in VPD headquarters with Bill Donaldson, Lyndon and Burke of the RCMP, and Peter. If the whisper-shouting, dilated pupils, frown, and tightness under his eyes were any indicators, Donaldson was furious. Lyndon stared over Donaldson's head, Burke looked mulish.

Diana placed a hand on Donaldson's arm. He looked at her and relaxed immediately. "Can you work your magic, Diana? He's here now. We've got nothing to lose, and maybe we'll get something *out of this mess.*" He spoke the last words through gritted teeth and glared at the two RCMPs.

Diana rolled her lips between her teeth. "I'll try."

"We'll watch you through the two-way."

"So, how do you want to do this?" Peter said. "The usual?"

"Not this time. I want you in the other room, watching, backing me up. Sergeant Major Lyndon can be in there with me." Diana turned to the RCMP man. "You stand behind Greene and slightly to the side. I want you just inside his peripheral vision. But you don't say a word, you understand? Just by standing there silently, you'll distract him enough so he can't give his full attention to controlling his expressions. It will make things go faster."

"This is a waste of time. He's not going to tell you anything. His lawyer won't let him say a word," Lyndon said.

"And whose fault is that?" Donaldson continued glaring at the other man. "Shut it. You'll do as you're told. If anyone can get him to talk, Diana can," Donaldson said.

The disbelief Lyndon felt showed on his face, along with a slice of barely concealed contempt. *How nice.* But it didn't matter. It was better. The more hostility Lyndon exuded, the more uncomfortable Greene would be.

"I don't need him to talk," Diana said with a smirk. "But I will need the list of events that are potential targets."

"Here," Lyndon said, handing her the file he was holding. Diana wanted to slap the look of scorn off his face, but there were more important things at stake than the man's condescension right now.

"Thank you," she said. "Peter, give me about twenty minutes, then come in and hand me a note. Look pleased, okay?"

"What note? Why?" Lyndon asked.

"You'll see." Diana squared her shoulders. "Let's get to it."

Lyndon grudgingly opened the door to the interrogation room and let her through. She nodded to him in thanks and walked in. "Hello, Mr. Greene," she said as she took the seat opposite. His lawyer sat next to him.

"Who the hell are you?" the lawyer demanded.

Diana raised an eyebrow. "Watch your tone," she snapped. "I'm Diana Hunter. I consult for VPD. And you are?"

"James Willoughby," the lawyer scoffed. "My client has nothing to say. The Vancouver Police Department is overstepping its bounds. Mr. Greene was arrested for no reason. You have absolutely nothing on him. This is an illegal arrest. Expect us to sue the RCMP and VPD." Willoughby was on a roll. But he was also concerned. His wide eyes and raised eyebrows told Diana so. The lawyer got to his feet and nodded to Greene, who rose alongside him.

"Sit down," Diana said calmly.

"You have no right to keep my client here."

"Mr. Greene, I suggest you sit," Diana repeated in a cool voice.

Greene looked torn, but something in Diana's face must have suggested that he'd better do as he was told. "Sit down, James," he said to his lawyer.

"I'm advising you against this, Riley. Don't say a word," the lawyer said.

"Mr. Greene doesn't have to tell me anything if he doesn't want to."

Lyndon had taken up position behind Greene, just as Diana had asked. The politician kept trying to look behind him.

"Mr. Greene!" Diana rapped her knuckles sharply on the tabletop. "You might not want to talk to us, but you will at least do me the courtesy of looking my way when I speak," she snapped. The man's gaze swiveled to her instantly.

"Is your name Riley Greene?" Diana asked.

"Yes," Greene replied automatically. The lawyer said nothing.

"Are you a Canadian senator?"

"Yes." Again, the lawyer didn't say a word.

"Do you like dogs?"

"Yes."

"Are you a Maple Leafs fan?" Diana said.

"No."

"Are you a Canucks fan?"

"Absolutely."

"What is this?" the lawyer demanded.

"Mr. Willoughby, I suggest you keep quiet, or I will have you removed from the room."

"How dare you? You can't do that!" Willoughby exclaimed.

"Your client has ties to a terrorist organization, and I'm not here representing VPD, I'm here representing CSIS, and I assure you, we can do that. So I suggest you keep your comments to yourself."

"This is Canada! You can't just go around accusing people, picking them up off the street as you see fit. My client has rights! And CSIS has no power here."

"Mr. Willoughby, you seem to be a little behind on the law, which has given CSIS a mandate, namely to reduce threats to the security of Canada, *by any means necessary*."

"You need approval from a judge."

"That's true *if* I were holding him against his will, but since all I'm doing is asking your client questions *that he is not obliged to answer*," Diana slowed down, emphasizing her words, "and you haven't left yet, don't you think you're getting a little overexcited? Mr. Greene is free to go if he chooses. Unless, of course, you *want* me to get a special order from a judge to keep Mr. Greene here."

"No judge will agree to something like that. Not for a Canadian *senator*." Willoughby was looking a little uncertain.

"Does that make him above the law? And do you want to test that theory?"

"Shut up, James!" Greene snapped.

"That's a smart move, Mr. Greene, very smart. Now that we've sorted that out, let's get on with it. Are you planning a bombing somewhere in Canada?"

Greene sputtered. "Of course not!"

Diana tipped her head. She watched him carefully. Greene's look of scorn was followed by a tiny flicker of a smile. "You're telling the truth. Interesting. You're good, Mr. Greene. I see I will have to take more care when formulating my questions. Well then, are you *aware* of a plan for a bombing somewhere in Canada?"

"No." Greene shook his head, but then he rubbed his throat and held his breath for a split second. No one would have noticed but Diana.

She smiled. "Lie. Thank you, Mr. Greene. Now, did you pay ILIF ten million dollars?"

"No, I did not pay ILIF ten million dollars," Greene replied. No contractions or word repetition. His words were accompanied by a one-sided shoulder shrug. His arms were crossed, and he leaned back. He might as well have had a neon sign over his head with an arrow pointing downward, the word "LIAR" spelled out in red.

"That's a lie," Diana said.

"What? Of course, it is not," Greene said.

"You didn't ask what ILIF is."

"They are some terrorist organization in the Middle East. It is not a secret. I have been briefed on them," Greene replied.

"That surprises me, Mr. Greene. They've only recently landed on the security forces' radar, and you are not cleared for the level of intelligence briefing that would be required to hear of them. ILIF has very little visibility at the moment since they haven't done anything truly spectacular. But that can change with your help. In fact, you're putting them on the map, aren't you? Very clever, Mr. Greene. Now, back to my questions," Diana said.

Interestingly, to Diana at least, Greene didn't display any shame whatsoever. He seemed pleased. "Did you pay ILIF the money so they would take responsibility for the bombing?"

"Are you crazy? Read my lips. I do not know about any bombing." Greene put his hand to his hair. He was red-faced and on the verge of shouting. But it was his tiny, almost imperceptible micro-expressions that were telling Diana everything she needed to know.

"And that's another lie. Mr. Greene. You're being extra-ordinarily helpful, thank you. Now, I'm going to read a list of events and dates. You will tell me if any of these are the target."

"I will do no such thing!"

Diana cocked her head. "I thought you didn't know anything about any bombing."

"I just meant I cannot tell you about something of which I am not aware." Greene scratched his cheek.

"Another lie. How interesting. Now, let's move on." Diana slowly recited the list of potential targets and their dates. She had memorized them and didn't take her eyes off the man across the table from her as she spoke. He never said a word, but he didn't have to. His face and body language was enough. He sat impassive and confident as she read out the whole list.

None of them triggered him. Greene didn't know where or when the bombing would happen.

CHAPTER TWENTY-ONE

"**N**OW, MR. GREENE, do you know how this attack will be carried out?"

"I don't know anything about this supposed attack."

Diana pressed on. "Will bombs be planted at the location?"

Greene said nothing but pressed his lips together. Diana noticed a fleeting expression of contempt followed by a tiny smile. She had it wrong.

"Will there be suicide bombers?"

Again, stony silence was the only response, but a slight sheen was appearing at Greene's hairline.

"I'll take that as a yes, then. Do you know who the bombers are?"

"You are crazy," Greene shouted at her. "Why would I do such a thing? Why would I hurt my own people?"

"That's an interesting reference, Mr. Greene. Do they belong to you? Your people." Diana arched one eyebrow. She abruptly changed tack. "What are their names, the suicide bombers?" She looked him straight in the eye, as though she were asking him what he wanted for dinner.

"That's enough! You've harassed my client *enough*!" Willoughby jumped to his feet.

Diana stood, too. She glared at Willoughby. "Sit down and keep your mouth shut, or I will ask Sergeant Major Lyndon to throw you back into that chair, if not out of the room."

Lyndon stepped forward prepared to follow her instructions. Willoughby sat down, frustrated and intimidated, muttering about *"the law."* At that moment, there was a knock on the door. Peter walked in, smirking. He handed Diana a piece of paper. She opened the folded note and nodded in approval. *Make him cry*, it said. Donaldson had signed it. Peter walked out of the room.

Diana looked up. "Well, Mr. Greene. It seems we no longer need your assistance. Instead, my colleague here will take you into custody. You will be remanded to Kent prison, where you will be questioned further and, in time no doubt, await your trial." Diana got up from the table.

"Wait! What are you talking about?" Greene exclaimed from his chair.

His lawyer banged his fists on the table. "This is outrageous! You have nothing on my client. All you have are a bunch of suppositions. You can't *arrest* him, let alone imprison him."

Diana cocked an eyebrow. "We have Mr. Bernard Kloch in custody. Remember him? Of Blue Panther Securities? He's accepted a deal." It was a lie, and it was entrapment, but Diana didn't care. The stakes were too high. She looked at Greene, assessing his response to her words. "He gave you up, Mr. Greene, and he has agreed to give us a list of all the details relating to your plan. He claims that a bombing was all your idea and that despite his protests, you insisted. He was merely the enabler."

Greene's eyes widened. "No, you are lying. You have to be. Kloch would never . . . I don't know—. It's all him. It's all on him!"

"Shut up, Riley!" Willoughby snapped.

Diana smiled. "Kloch would never what, Mr. Greene?"

"Riley, don't say anything," Willoughby warned.

"Oh for God's sake, James, shut up! Can't you see they already know everything? This is my only chance to cut a deal!"

"They're just fishing! And now you're giving them everything, you fool!"

Greene looked back and forth between Willoughby and Diana. "How do I know you're not lying?" he asked Diana, squinting.

Diana rolled her eyes. "Mr. Greene, that's the thing. You don't. That's a risk you are going to have to take. But as you've practically admitted your involvement in this horrible scheme, it would appear that you don't have anything to lose. In any case, we aren't dependent upon your help." Diana was good at lying. She knew all the tricks. "We already have the cake, and very good cake it is, too. You are merely the icing. However, I'm not sure I would want to take a fall thanks to Kloch. Ho hum." She turned and headed for the door.

Lyndon walked over. "Stand up, Mr. Greene."

"No, you can't do this!" he shouted.

Diana opened the door, then turned back. "I can. But I must remember to publicly thank you for your help. Everyone will know precisely how cooperative you've been."

Greene paled. He went from outrage and fear to terror.

Diana left the room. Donaldson was waiting for her in the corridor. "What are you doing? We need names and addresses," he hissed.

"Wait for it, wait for it—"

Right on cue, Greene started screaming through the door. "Ms. Hunter! Ms. Hunter! Please! Come back! I'll tell you what I know! Everything!"

Diana grinned at Donaldson, who shook his head. "I don't know why I was worried," he grumbled.

Diana schooled her features and went back into the room. A glance at Lyndon made her want to smile. He was looking at her with awe. She pushed a notepad and pen toward Greene. "Start writing, Mr. Greene. I want a full confession and specifics. I want dates, locations, and times. Leave nothing out, understand? You give me all the information you have and I'll speak to the Attorney General on your behalf."

"I don't know . . . I don't know much," Greene asserted.

Diana raised her eyebrows and reached out to slide the notepad back toward her. Greene's hand shot out. He placed his fingertips on the pad.

"I overheard a name being mentioned once. That's all I know. Kloch kept me out of it."

"Give."

"What about protection?" he whispered.

Diana nodded. Greene took the pen and wrote. He slid the paper back to her. She spun it around and read.

"Chakrib. Mosque on 8th Avenue."

In the viewing room, Burke dialed a number. "Mosque on 8th. Chakrib. Now."

"That's all I know, I promise. I had no hand in the details," Greene said.

"Are you certain? You don't know when? Where?

"I don't know when, and I don't know what."

Willoughby was red in the face. "He'll never be convicted. Everything you've done is against procedure. I'll have this case thrown out of court faster than you can sneeze!"

"Really? That's all you care about? You don't care that your client knew about a plan to bomb this country and kill hundreds, possibly thousands of people?" Diana's eyes were wide as she surveyed the attorney from her chair across the table. "Seriously, Mr. Willoughby, your defense of your client is lamentable in the circumstances. But seeing as we're arguing semantics, what procedures have I breached?" Diana asked.

"I told you my client wouldn't speak to you, but you ignored me. That's a violation of his rights!"

"Really? I don't remember forcing him to speak. I clearly remember stating that he didn't need to tell me anything. And he didn't, did he? Isn't that so, Sergeant Major?"

"Yes, ma'am," Lyndon replied, his tone respectful. Extremely respectful compared to the hostility he'd exhibited earlier.

Diana regarded the attorney coolly. "Anyhow, that's all beside the point now. My objective is met. I suggest you leave things there." Willoughby opened his mouth and then slammed it shut, glaring at her. He looked ready to rip her head off. "Mr. Willoughby, I've been playing this game a very long time. Now, if you'll excuse me, I have work to do. Other officers will be in to take a detailed statement from your client."

Diana left the room with Lyndon on her heels. Donaldson and Peter were waiting for her. "Nicely done, Diana. As usual," Donaldson said with a grin. "I'll send people out for Kloch. Burke has already sent someone to pick this Chakrib fellow up."

"We'll swarm the mosque and start interviewing everyone in connection with it," Lyndon said.

"No," Peter intervened.

"We have to!"

"If you go in heavy like that, they'll get wind of it and run. They'll melt off the face of the earth. Let's quietly get this Chakrib guy and get the intel we need from him. Then we can swarm."

CHAPTER TWENTY-TWO

MALCOLM BERESFORD LEANED over and quickly took his last gulp of tea before dropping his mug into the sink with a clatter. He was running late for work. Normally, he liked to get up early and miss the crowds, but he'd slept in this morning, exhausted after being repeatedly awoken by his four-year-old daughter's coughing and his wife's ministrations. He blearily shrugged on his jacket and grabbed his computer bag. Hopefully, he could sneak out before any of the others woke up. He had a lot to get done and only half a day to do it. The SkyTrain would be packed.

"Daddy!"

Malcolm cringed as his six-year-old son, Dean, ran up behind him, his fleecy Spiderman onesie rustling as he padded along. The blond hair on the back of his head was all mussed and needed a good combing. In his hands, Dean clutched a plastic case filled with trading cards along with a well-worn, brown teddy bear, its fur matted and even bare in places.

"Daddy, it's today! Today!"

"I know, buddy. Looking forward to it?" Malcolm ruffled the boy's hair, making it stand up even more.

"I can't wait! They're gonna do it, Daddy! They're gonna do it!" Dean held his hands aloft, his bear jiggling above his head as he jumped up and down.

"Let's hope so, bud. We'll find out tonight, huh?"

The Canucks were in the Stanley Cup playoffs for the first time in years. It had been a big surprise for the whole of Vancouver. The team had played badly in the run-up, but now the entire city was enthralled. Streets emptied, bars filled, and friends held impromptu parties each time one of the games took place. They were playing the Toronto Maple Leafs in the finals. It was the first time in nearly thirty years that two Canadian teams had made it through. It had transfixed the entire country. Tonight, the Canucks could clinch the series.

Malcolm, a lifelong and passionate hockey fan, had paid a fortune to score a couple of tickets from a co-worker who'd had a family emergency at the last minute. He'd planned to get a babysitter so he and his wife, Stella, could attend the game, but his daughter's sickness had meant he'd asked Dean if he'd like to go instead. Malcolm would miss enjoying the event with Stella, but he'd get some quality father-son bonding time, something he didn't get enough of, given his work schedule. Together, they'd make some exceptional memories, he figured.

Dean, not usually interested in sports, had picked up on his father's excitement and developed a fast and unswerving obsession with the game over the past few days. He'd memorized the players' names and watched all the playoff games the Canucks had played to this point. He'd become mesmerized by the fast-moving action and the player's skills, and while he didn't understand all the rules, he understood enough to know that a goal for his team was a good thing.

Malcolm and Dean were leaving for the stadium at 2 p.m. If the team was successful, they might even join the crowds in the streets afterward, although Stella was keen for them to make their way home right away. Dean held out the trading cards in his hands.

"Test me?"

"Not now, bud, I've got to go to work, but I'll be back in time for us to go to the match. We don't want to miss the start of the game, do we?"

Dean tipped his head back, dropped his shoulders, and pursed his lips. "Okaaay," he said. "But what am I gonna do 'til then?"

"Mama will take you to school. Then when you come home and have gotten dressed, it'll be time to go. The time will pass quickly, you'll see."

Malcolm hastily poured Dean some cereal and sloshed milk into the bowl. He had a meeting to attend and a report to write up. If he were lucky, he'd get a seat on the train and catch up on his emails. There'd be no time for lunch or even a coffee. He plonked the cereal down on the table and washed his hands.

Dean scrambled up onto a chair and engaged in some vigorous slurping, his head bent deep to the bowl. Malcolm looked over at him and stopped for a moment as he hoisted the strap of his laptop bag onto his shoulder. He wanted to fix this picture in his memory; his small, fair-haired son in his Spiderman pajamas, his teddy bear now face down on the table next to him, the trading cards strewn around the floor. Malcolm blinked a couple of times before kissing the top of Dean's head and dashing out of the door.

Sunlight shone brightly on Salah's face. He squinted and covered his eyes with his hands. The slatted bedroom blind letting in the early morning light had broken years ago, and they'd never had the money or the will to fix it. Every summer morning, the sun would awaken Salah by shining directly into the room and onto his face as soon as it peeked above the horizon. There was rarely any need for him to set an alarm. Besides, there was nothing in particular to get up for.

Salah lay there, thinking. He could hear his father snoring in a room down the hallway, and he could see the arm of his younger brother dangling from the bunk above. The other bed in the room was empty. His older brother, Ismaël had not come home last night. Salah searched under his pillow for his phone and checked the time. His mother would be on her way from her night shift at a local bakery to her early morning shift cleaning bathrooms at a local high school. Salah sighed and rubbed his eyes.

He threw the thin blanket back and shrugged on pants and a sweatshirt. Scratching his back and yawning, he made his way to the kitchen. Salah was measuring coffee into the espresso maker when he heard his father call out to him. A flash of anger ran through him like lightning, fast and hot. Salah carried on spooning coffee into the pot, focusing extra hard to crowd out the hopelessness he felt in the face of his father's overwhelming needs. His hand shook, and he spilled coffee grounds on the countertop.

He heard his father call his name again. Salah shut his eyes tightly and pressed his full lips into a thin line, willing his mind blank. He leaned against the laminate counter. *When would this stop? When would this ever stop?* His father moaned. Salah threw the spoon noisily into the coffee pot and was gone, running down the hallway and into the street outside.

Two sturdy and unyielding RCMP officers manhandled the man through the doors of the nondescript industrial unit they'd brought him to. The prisoner had a long wiry dark beard punctuated with gray. It fell to the middle of his chest. His head was shaved. The lack of hair up top and the profusion of it on his chin drew attention to his scarred nose and deep brown eyes. He wore his pajamas—a gray V-neck t-shirt and striped cotton pants—and dirty slides on his feet. There were cuffs around his wrists.

The man had been pulled from his bed, and he was not happy. He resisted the officer's demands just enough to show his defiance, roughly shrugging his shoulders when they gripped his arms to propel him forward. The Mounties said nothing to him, their navy combat gear and weapons demonstrating all he needed to know about who they were and why they were there.

"I can do it," he growled as he sat down on the cheap plastic chair in the middle of the room. On the floor was a length of rope. In the corner, there was a bin liner and some discarded plastic gloves. The floor was filthy. Incongruously, a fringed lampshade more suited to an eighties living room hung from the ceiling.

The two RCMP officers stood guard by the door and the man on the chair slumped to the side like a moody teenager. He was in no hurry. There was nowhere he needed to be. He had done his part. Now, all Mohammed Chakrib had to do was wait.

CHAPTER TWENTY-THREE

C HAKRIB WAS DOZING in his chair when he was awoken by the sound of a car outside. Two doors slammed, and he heard brisk footsteps approach the building. The pair spoke quietly; he made out a woman's voice along with that of a man. Chakrib stirred, his face twisting into a grim smile. The door to the building opened.

"Mr. Chakrib, how are you?"

Chakrib grunted. He looked the woman over. She was tall, youngish, about thirty, he guessed, attractive, and slim. She was dressed in brown cargo pants and a black, long-sleeved, crew-neck t-shirt. Over the top was a Kevlar vest that he guessed hid her automatic weapon. The guy was dressed the same except his shirt was short-sleeved, revealing an impressive upper arm musculature that pointed to the fact that he worked out regularly. They both held bottles of water.

"My name is Diana, and this is my partner, Peter. I'm sorry these gentlemen had to get you up in the middle of the night, but we have important work to do. I hope your wife wasn't too disturbed. I did ask them to be quiet so as not to wake your children." Chakrib, who was still lounging on the chair, looked at her and raised his handcuffed wrists.

"You want out of the cuffs?" Diana turned to Peter. "What do you think? Should we let Mr. Chakrib out of his restraints?" Peter shrugged. "With four of us here, I think that should be okay," she continued. An RCMP officer moved forward. Chakrib offered his wrists and dropped his hands in his lap once they were released.

"Would you like some water?" Diana asked brightly. Again, Chakrib grunted. She passed him her bottle. He took a long drink and offered it back to her.

Diana raised her hand. "No, please. You keep it." She nodded to the two RCMP officers standing by the door. "Have your two keepers here been nice to you?"

Chakrib ignored her. He was stalling. He knew how the game was played. First, they asked you inane questions or made small talk to gauge your responses. Then they asked you about what they really wanted to know and judged your reactions in comparison. Chakrib wasn't planning on giving them a helping hand. He would say as little as possible. Even if things got dirty. *All he had to do was wait.*

"How many children do you have, Mohammed? Five, isn't it? Two boys and three girls?" Diana was standing, but she bent down and showed Chakrib a photo of his family. It had been taken in the backyard around two months ago. *How had they gotten that?* He followed the image with his eyes as the woman stood again and tucked it in her back pocket. "They'll be getting up for school soon, right?" She was fishing.

"Now, we've heard rumors about you being involved in plans for a bombing. What can you tell me about that,

Mohammed?" Chakrib said nothing. He didn't meet her eyes as he continued to ignore her.

"Mohammed? Do you have anything to say to me?" He felt his foot move as she gently kicked it to get his attention. He wasn't going to talk to this Western female piece of—

"Chakrib!" It was the guy now, not so pleasant. "Look at her when she speaks to you. It's only polite."

Chakrib lazily raised his eyes to look at Peter. He shifted slightly in his seat. The woman appeared in his field of vision again.

"There's a bombing planned. Your name came up in connection with it." Still silence.

Chakrib stared at Diana, and as he closed his eyes to blink, he swiveled in his seat to turn away from her. "You don't know how corrupt your government is." He was mumbling.

"What? What's that?" Diana seized on his words.

"You don't know how corrupt your government *is*!" Chakrib yelled the final word at her, spinning around in the chair.

"Then tell me. Tell me, Mohammed, tell me for the sake of your children. They'll be hurt by this, too." Diana leaned in to press home her point. An error. Chakrib turned quickly and spat at her. Spittle landed on Diana's cheek.

Peter immediately stepped in and put his face menacingly close to Chakrib's. "Do that again, and you *will* regret it. Now, we have been nice to you. It's time for you to be nice to us." Chakrib glowered at him from below bushy eyebrows.

Diana tried again. "Tell me about the bombing that you've planned." Chakrib turned away from her. "Mohammed, look at me when I'm talking to you." Chakrib smiled and languidly spun on his seat so that he was facing her again.

Diana repeated her question. "What do you know about a planned bombing?" Chakrib looked at the ceiling, refusing any attempt from Diana to make eye contact. "Your children like it here, don't they Mohammed? They have their friends, their phones, a good education."

Chakrib's eyes hardened. "It would be a shame if all that came to an end, wouldn't it?" Chakrib's eyelids dropped and his face relaxed. He said nothing.

Diana changed tack. "Tell me about the bombing. When is it planned for? This month?" Chakrib looked at her insolently. "This week?" Nothing. "Today?"

There was the tiniest flicker around Chakrib's mouth. Peter noticed it, too. *Oh boy.*

"Where is it going to take place, Mohammed?" Diana asked.

The big man chuckled, revealing yellow, crooked teeth. He folded his arms. He looked over at Peter, and back at Diana, his face full of contempt.

Hours later, Peter and Diana stepped outside the building. The light cast shadows in the mid-afternoon sunshine. Diana wiped the sweat from her brow and leaned against the outside wall. She put the heels of her hands into her eye sockets.

Peter walked away from the building, rolling the stiffness from his shoulders before turning on his phone and making a call. He spoke briefly. He walked back to where Diana stood and leaned against the wall next to her.

"I just called Donaldson and updated him. He's going

to brief Lyndon. They're going to quietly pick off a few of Chakrib's known associates to see what they know. There's no sign of Kloch, he must have gone to ground."

"We're getting nowhere in there. We haven't learned a thing. He's stalling something mighty fine. Not even a veiled threat to his family was effective. He's been trained well." Diana sighed. "What do you think?"

"Something is about to go down, I'm sure of it. I'm betting that Chakrib knows that if he stalls long enough, the plan, whatever it is, will be put into action. I'm worried that it's today."

"I think it's today, too. Did you see the change when I mentioned it?" Peter nodded. "So let's think. What are our options?"

"We could turn this guy over to someone else, see if they have more luck. We could keep doing what we are doing and hope we wear him down. We could get the RCMP to interrogate his associates and hope we find someone more amenable. Or . . . " Peter looked pointedly at Diana, hesitant to mention what he'd been considering. "We could up the ante."

"No! No! Seriously, Peter! I can't believe you would even suggest it!"

"Diana, we don't have much time." Peter spread his hands. "This is a massive threat, and Chakrib is a big player. This isn't some playboy in a luxury hotel room. Chakrib's a maniac. He doesn't care about anyone, not even his own family. And he holds the lives of hundreds, maybe thousands of civilians in his hands. You know as well as I do that in these circumstances, with us facing such a big threat, possibly within a very short timeframe, other authorities wouldn't hesitate. In this case, the ends *would* justify the means."

"I can't."

"You wouldn't have to."

"Would you?"

Peter hesitated before inclining his head slightly. "I might. If I felt it was the only way." Diana stared at him.

"And you think we're at that point now?"

"I think we're dangerously close."

Diana banged her head against the wall behind her. "We *have* to find another way."

"The clock is ticking. We can't wait much longer. For all we know, suicide bombers are making their way to their target as we speak."

"I know that!"

"Okay, what do you suggest?"

"He knows something, a lot. He wasn't giving anything away in there, but I'm convinced of it. We have to get it out of him."

"Okay, and do what? Straightforward interrogation isn't working, you've threatened his family, and he has his expressions down pat."

"Why don't we go counter-intuitive? Befriend him. Get his guard down. The 'coffee and a cigarette' approach."

"Diana, that takes time we don't have. Look, I understand your revulsion, but we have to move fast."

Diana fell silent, watching him. Peter paced the hard ground, chewing his lip, hands on his hips once more. He stopped and stared hard at a crack in the dust. "We don't have a choice." He looked up at her.

"What will you do?"

"There's a hose and running water in the room. I have a towel in my gym bag. It's in the car."

Diana turned away. "I don't want any part of this."

"Okay, stay outside," he said evenly.

Diana watched Peter walk to his car to retrieve the towel. He turned back, his face grim.

"Wait for me. I'll be back out in a bit."

Peter strode past her. Diana didn't look at him as she stared across the rough ground. The door to the building closed with a clang.

"Wait!" Diana suddenly called out. "I'm with you. You don't want this any more than I do."

CHAPTER TWENTY-FOUR

P ETER ORDERED THE two RCMP officers from
the room. Chakrib's eyes darted around looking at
Diana and Peter in turn. He sensed the uptick in
the atmosphere, but he remained silent.

When the two men had left, Peter moved to put the
handcuffs back on Chakrib. He was clinical and focused.
He tied Chakrib's legs to the chair. He moved over to the
hose that lay on the floor. He traced it back to a tap hidden
under a pile of detritus in the corner. He turned it a quarter
turn clockwise and a slow stream of water started to trickle
from the nozzle.

He showed it to Chakrib. "Are you sure there's nothing
you want to say to us, Mohammed? Because I sure would
rather not do this. And I'm sure you would rather I didn't,
too." Chakrib said nothing, although his arrogant effect of
earlier was more subdued now.

"Tip his head back," Peter told Diana. Diana moved to
stand behind Chakrib and took his head in her hands. As
she tipped it back to a forty-five-degree angle, he didn't
resist.

Peter picked up the towel he'd retrieved from his car and folded it in half. "Look, this isn't going to be pleasant for any of us. You know that after a few minutes, you'll be singing, so why don't you cut out the middle and tell us what we want to know now?"

Peter straddled Chakrib's knees and looked him in the eye. "Last chance."

Chakrib stared back at him as Peter draped the towel over the man's face, covering it entirely—his eyes, his nose, his mouth. Running water was pooling on the floor. Peter looked up at Diana.

"Are you sure about this?" she said.

"Yes, are you?"

"Yes."

"Ready?"

"Ready."

There was silence in the room. All they could hear were the birds overhead and Chakrib's breathing. Diana's hands were shaking. She had a feeling of dread pressing like a lead weight against her chest. Peter leaned over, the hose in his right hand.

A ringtone pealed through the air. Diana whipped her phone from her pocket, letting go of Chakrib's head momentarily before placing her arm across his forehead and pressing down hard.

"Yes?" She listened as Peter waited. "Yes, sir. We're on our way!" Diana scrabbled to get her phone back into her pocket and ripped the towel off Chakrib's face. "We don't need you anymore, sunshine." She turned to Peter. "That was Donaldson. They got a tip-off. We're the nearest. We've got to go."

Peter tossed the hose back into the corner. He turned to Chakrib, "You got lucky. Have a good think about your situation while you're on a break. You might not be so fortunate next time."

The pair ran to the car. Diana plugged the address Donaldson had given her into her phone. They were seven minutes away. Her phone pinged.

"What are they saying?" Peter asked her as he strapped himself in.

Diana read the message on her screen. "Suspicious activity increasing in the last few hours. Middle Eastern. Apartment is leased to an Omar Lazez and his wife. Bomb squad and armed tactical units are on their way."

"Do we know how many suspects we're dealing with?"

"No."

Peter swore as he tore the car around a corner. He was fueled up on adrenaline and frustration that had been building for hours now, but when they got to the address, he took his foot off the gas and drove the car slowly past the apartment building to survey the scene.

The apartment was located in a bland seventies housing block built from concrete. Bright orange wooden paneling was tacked on at intervals, obviously to relieve the plain aspect. Outside a young mother wearing a hijab chatted on her phone. She rocked a brown curly-haired toddler in a buggy back and forth as she spoke. A few yards away, a group of Asian youths hung around a bus shelter. They appeared intent on not very much, least of all catching a bus. Peter drove on. He parked the car half a block away from the address they'd been given.

"We walk from here." Peter took Diana's hand, and they walked down the street like any other couple. The sidewalk was interspersed with lampposts thirty yards apart and in between them were large, raised wooden planters. Sparse, moribund bushes dotted with occasional purple flowers grew inside them.

Peter glanced upward. There was a man at the window of an apartment. He looked to be in his early thirties, his dark-skinned face expressionless as he stared at the scene below. Peter heard sirens.

Two police cars pulled up sharply outside the building. Behind it, an armored vehicle drew to a stop. Further away, more police cars arrived and barricaded the street. Peter turned and saw the exercise repeated in the other direction. Armed officers streamed from the vehicles to take up position, guns readied.

Peter looked back at the man in the window. His face was impassive, but he stood to attention, his body rigid. The man brought his hand to the middle of his chest...

"Get down!" Peter turned to push Diana against a brick wall. He covered her with his body and flinched as glass was blown into the street, shards raining down on the sidewalk, smoke and flames billowing out from the apartment above them. The boom of the explosion reached them in less than a second. It was followed closely by the updraft as the vacuum created by the explosion was refilled, the wind dragging back debris and shrapnel from the blast with it.

There was a moment of stunned silence. Leaves floated noiselessly down from the sky. A whine was followed by a rustle as a tree branch fell harmlessly to the ground. Then, screaming.

The sound of a baby crying could be heard from an apartment. The stroller that a moment ago had carried a toddler was on its side, the child still strapped in, stunned but blinking and apparently unharmed. His mother was on the ground, unconscious but alive, blood from a head wound running down her face, her hand still clutching her phone.

Peter looked over to where the youths had been standing at the bus stop. Three of them had been blown across the street and were stirring, but the bodies of two more lay unmoving. One was trapped between the bus shelter and a wall. The other knelt on the sidewalk, his cheek laying on a bus shelter seat, his arms dangling, as though he were taking a rest.

Diana reached up and caught a torn scrap of paper that was wafting slowly down when a movement in her peripheral vision caught her attention. "There!"

She started down an alleyway that ran along the side of the apartment block. A man was ahead of her. Peter followed. Diana was fast, but Peter was bigger and stronger. He quickly closed in on her and took over the chase. The pursuant was young, lithe, and light on his feet, but he was no match for Peter.

Peter chased the man down the side of the apartments and across the road, taking steps down to an underpass two and three at a time. He was closing fast, sprinting through the tunnel, splashing through puddles that had congregated in the gloominess.

As Peter caught up, he reached out to grab the man's shoulders and shoved him against graffiti sprayed on the side of the tunnel, his hips pinning the man against the concrete, his palm forcing his captive's face roughly against the wall.

"Don't shoot, don't shoot." The man in Peter's firm hold was wide-eyed. His hands were up. Adrenaline coursed through both of their veins.

Peter tore his captive's hands behind his back and

cuffed him. "Turn around!" He grabbed the man's shoulder and forced him around. "Sit!"

Diana ran up to join them. She crouched. "What's your name? What's going on?"

"No, no. I can't say, I can't say. They will kill me."

"Who will kill you?"

"No, no."

Peter elbowed his way past Diana and grabbed the man's shirt. Moments after making him sit, Peter pulled the man to standing, his face inches away and menacing. "Look pal, the jig's up. Your friend up there just blew himself to smithereens and took several people with him. This isn't going to get any better for you."

Peter managed to get his words out in between deep breaths. He was still panting. He let go, and the man dropped to the ground and buried his head between his knees.

When the man began to rock and wail, Peter drove an arm under his armpits and hauled him to his feet once more. "I've had just about enough of people refusing to talk to me today. You *will* tell me what's up. You're part of a terrorist cell, aren't you?"

The man shook his head. "Driver. That's all. No bombing." Peter eyed him skeptically. "I swear, I swear. I was told to come to this address. I was to pick up three people."

"And take them where?" The man didn't reply. "And take them *where*?" Peter grabbed the man's shirt and shook him.

"The stadium," Diana said.

Peter looked at her. "What?"

"The playoff game," She was staring at the paper she had caught earlier. It was a ticket. "Starts at five o'clock."

Peter looked at his watch. It was 4:30 p.m.

Malcolm carried Dean the last part of the way. The six-year-old was flagging. It had taken them two hours to make their way from their home, through the public transit system, and down toward the stadium, a journey that normally took forty minutes. There was just half an hour left until the start of the game and the crush of the crowd was at its peak.

"Are we there yet?" Dean asked.

"We're close, son," his father said, panting a little with the effort it took to keep up with the crowd and carry his son. "Look, it's ahead of us. Can you see?" He pointed to the Rogers Arena. It held a capacity crowd of 19,000 and today it would be full.

Dean craned his neck to look at the flat, cylindrical building. "It looks like a spaceship!"

"Eh?" Malcolm looked ahead. "I suppose it does. Like from Star Wars." He was glad for a way to perk up his son and distract him from what had been, for a six-year-old, and even a thirty-eight-year-old, an arduous journey.

Malcolm reflected that he had tried to do too much. He should have taken the day off or worked from home. He should have leisurely made his way to the game with Dean and made a day of it. Going to work, then rushing home again, only to go out again immediately, had been overly optimistic and put them all under more stress than was necessary. Even Malcolm was beginning to flag, and the game hadn't even started yet.

CHAPTER TWENTY-FIVE

"**D**ADDY!" DEAN HAD come running down the hallway when Malcolm arrived home. The boy was all decked out in his Canucks gear. He was wearing his blue, green, and white hockey shirt that had a player's name and number on the back. On his head, a matching beanie emblazoned with the Canuck whale logo was covering his ears.

Malcolm's morning at work hadn't gone well. As Marketing Vice President of the start-up he worked for, he'd had an important meeting with his CEO. The company was getting ready for a new round of venture capital. They were running out of cash and needed the funding badly. It had been critical that Malcolm prepare his boss for the questions he would get from potential investors, but his CEO had not taken easily to being tutored.

Malcolm momentarily closed his eyes to shut out the prospect of what would happen if the company didn't get the funding. He reminded himself instead to focus on having a great time with Dean at the match. If the Canucks won, everything else would get forgotten for a while. "Hi, bud. All ready?"

Malcolm looked at Stella for an answer. His wife nodded. She was leaning up against the kitchen counter, her arms folded, smiling. She looked as pretty as ever, even though she'd been up all night. Her dark hair softly curled around her face, her slim, trim figure and long legs draped in a flowery wraparound dress. She had old, worn, furry slippers, once a pale pink, on her feet. "How's Alice? Is she any better?"

"She'll live. She's napping now, so Dean and I had some time to get ready." Stella looked at the clock. "If you leave now, I might even get a few minutes to myself before she wakes up."

Malcolm turned back to Dean. "We have to leave quickly. Let me go and change, and then we'll be off, okay?"

"Yes!" the boy said. He lifted his arms in the air, fists clenched, and jumped up and down on the spot. Dean was fit to burst.

Malcolm rushed upstairs to throw his own Canucks jersey over a light fleece sweater and a pair of lined pants. He rolled on a pair of thick socks. As he raced out of the bedroom, heading for the garage, he heard a small voice. "Daddy." Malcolm turned on the stairs to see his three-year-old daughter standing on the landing, gazing down at him. She looked very small.

Alice had dark hair like her mother, but otherwise, she was the spitting image of Malcolm, and now she poked her head through the banister rails and gave him a small smile. She looked flushed and warm from sleep. She was wearing mismatched pajamas. There were flamingo legs printed on her bottoms while the top was adorned with the head of a unicorn. Regarding her through the railings, Malcolm realized how ill Alice must feel. She would never wear such an outfit under normal circumstances.

Malcolm pushed thoughts of leaving for the game from his mind and walked back up the stairs. He sat down on the top step and pulled Alice into his lap. She silently turned to face him and lay her head on his shoulder as he stroked her hair with one hand and supported her body with the other.

They sat there quietly for a while, Malcolm torn between relaxing into the moment with his daughter and his urgency to be on his way to the game with his son. Eventually, he peeled himself away from Alice and held her so he could look at her.

"I have to go, sweetheart." Alice rubbed her eyes and gave a little whimper. "Mommy will look after you. Let's go find her, eh?" He stood and carried Alice down the stairs.

"Ali needs her mama."

Malcolm walked into the kitchen where Stella was washing up. Stella's shoulders slumped a little at his words, but she turned around and wiped her hands on a towel before taking the girl, her arms outstretched, from her father.

"Okay, baby. Let's go and watch some TV, shall we?"

Malcolm walked impatiently behind them as Stella carried Alice down the hallway, and as soon as they'd peeled off into the living room, he dove through the internal door into the garage. There, he collected the final items he needed. Gloves, hat, sneakers. He was good.

Malcolm ran back into the kitchen and grabbed his son's hand and the backpack he'd prepared earlier. "Let's go!" They dashed out of the door. Dean clambered into his car seat and fastened himself in. Malcolm did the same, throwing his backpack onto the passenger seat.

"Damn!" Malcolm swore as he started the engine. He

paused for a second before undoing his seatbelt and sprinting back into the house, leaving the car engine running. When he came back, he threw a pair of ear defenders next to his pack. He didn't want a repeat of the last time he'd taken Dean to a game.

Dean had grizzled all through it, overwhelmed by the cold and the noise. They'd ended up leaving early, both of them in bad moods. Malcolm was hoping that the intervening four years had been long enough for Dean to mature so that he could withstand the chill and sound of a hockey match and be swept along by the excitement instead.

Malcolm and Stella had relocated to North Vancouver when Stella was pregnant with Dean. They'd considered it a more family-friendly neighborhood in which to bring up their children than the hipster downtown district they had lived in when they were first married.

They hadn't regretted it, but the downside was the commute into the city for work and events like this playoff game. It wasn't too bad by major city standards, but taking Dean into the city was a major undertaking for Malcolm, one he wasn't totally comfortable with. He had never felt completely at ease taking sole responsibility for his children and very much played second fiddle behind Stella's highly competent first violin in that regard.

From home, the father and son drove to the SeaBus terminal and took the ferry across the inner harbor of Burrard Inlet, the expanse of water that separated North Vancouver from the inner city. They had trudged off the ferry and stood waiting patiently on the platform for the SkyTrain to take them to their destination.

Around them were couples, families, groups of friends, all making the same pilgrimage into the city, most of them decked out in the blue, green, and white colors of the home team. Five trains passed, too full for them to squeeze onto. For Dean, the wait was interminable, but he'd stayed upbeat, his behavior holding up in the way of children who instinctively know when it matters.

Finally, they shuffled into a SkyTrain carriage and wedged themselves in. It was standing room only. Malcolm showed Dean how to hold on to a pole to steady himself and a few minutes later, the Chinatown-Stadium station came into view. They took the stairs down to the street.

"Can you pick up the pace, buddy?" Malcolm was getting concerned about the crowds. People were pushing, urging others on.

"Daddy, there's so many people."

Malcolm looked down at Dean's face, his eyes wide. "Yeah, I know, bud. Just get down the stairs and then we'll stop. I've got an idea."

Dean clambered down, stumbling a little as he took the steps too fast. The tread was too deep for a little guy at this speed. Malcolm kept a firm grip on his son's hand and more than once, kept Dean upright as the crowd jostled around them.

When the pair got to the foot of the stairs, they moved out to the side away from the crush, and Malcolm dropped his backpack from his shoulders. He put his arms through the straps so that the pack lay across his front and crouched down, stretching his arms out behind him.

"Up you get, Dean. All aboard!"

Dean put his hands on his father's shoulders and in one well-practiced move, Malcolm leaned forward and grabbed his son's thighs, shrugging to position him high on his back.

"All aboard!" Dean cried, used to this ritual. Rejuvenated, father and son marched down Expo Viaduct toward the stadium.

The crowd marching down the thoroughfare was diverse. A complete cross-section of Vancouver had come out for the match. There were families, couples, and groups of young men and women. There were children—Dean, at six years old, was certainly not unique—and seniors. The people in the crowd were there to support their team and enjoy themselves. They had a mission, and they would not be diverted from it.

"Okay, buddy. I've got to put you down for a sec." When Dean and Malcolm came to a stop, the crowd continued forward, barely checking their pace, swirling around them like eddies in a pool. Malcolm crouched, and Dean scrambled off his back.

Malcolm rummaged through his backpack for their tickets. As he dug around, he held his breath as he scolded himself for not securing them better. He opened every compartment, and when that didn't produce a result, ran his hand through the contents of the main section once more. He felt the fleece of a spare jacket, a pair of earbuds for his phone, a plastic bottle, the ear defenders he'd gone back for earlier, and an assortment of pens, candies, and wet wipes, along with the ubiquitous fluff and dirt.

"Aha, got them!" Malcolm cried triumphantly as his hand found the paper edges of the envelope containing the tickets. "Come on Dean, we're going in." He looked around, but all he could see was the legs of people around him. Adult people. "Dean? Dean?"

But Dean was gone.

CHAPTER TWENTY-SIX

S ALAH CLIMBED INTO the back of the BMW. Abdel was in the front passenger seat. Jawad was driving this time. He looked at Salah in the rearview mirror. "Alright?"

"Alright," Salah replied.

"How're you feeling?"

"Okay."

"Good. We're off." Jawad pulled away from the curb and drove carefully and methodically through the streets. Nothing he did drew anyone's attention.

"It's quiet."

"Yeah," Abdel replied. None of them offered an explanation as to why.

Salah stared out of the window at the passing scenery. He was apprehensive. They passed his old high school. Kids were playing on the basketball court. They looked like the boy he had once been but was no longer. After a few minutes, they turned into the Surrey Central SkyTrain parking lot and drove to the furthest corner. None of them got out of the car.

Ten minutes later, Salah felt himself relax. *Perhaps he wasn't coming.* But then a maroon car, a Japanese make, Salah didn't know which one—it hardly mattered—glided into the parking space next to them. The driver got out, opened the BMW's passenger door, and slid into the seat next to Salah. He was around thirty and swaggered a little. Close-set brown eyes darted around the car as he spoke softly, his full lips surrounded by neatly trimmed stubble. "Everyone feeling well?"

"Yes, Ibrahim," Abdel said.

"We're good, man," Jawad added. "We did as you said." Salah thought he sounded pathetic, ingratiating himself to the older man.

"What about you, Salah?" Ibrahim turned to look at the youngest of the group. "Are you well?"

Salah hesitated. "Sure, he's good," Abdel answered, a nerve twitching in his jaw.

"You remember why we are doing this?" Ibrahim's piercing gaze hardened. He focused on Salah who turned toward him but avoided looking Ibrahim in the eye. "This is a wonderful day, truly wonderful. You know that we have talked and talked, but they do not listen. Today, you will give value to all those who have used their words over and over and over again and yet have not been heard. Those who have been harmed, injured, left hopeless, and betrayed. You know that you will honor our brothers and sisters, yes?"

"Yes, Ibrahim." Salah's voice shook. He glanced at Ibrahim before looking away again.

"Are you sure, bro? Or are you scared? A little boy afraid? Wanting to run home to a mommy who is never there?" Abdel always had been a nasty piece of work, aggression and cruelty often streaming from his mouth. He sneered at the world, at the government, at the police, at others, at Salah. Salah knew that Abdel's anger was a projection of his own shame and impotence, but the force of it was hard to withstand. Wavy, shoulder-length hair framed Abdel's face, and now he pulled down the sun visor, arranging it in the mirror. He turned in his seat so Salah could see his profile. *Peacock.*

"Shut up, Abdel! We are soldiers, Salah, and this is our war. We fight the infidels with all we have in vengeance for those they have killed and maimed. May they taste their own blood this day. Do you hear me?" Ibrahim said. There was a pause. "Salah?"

"I hear you," Salah replied quietly.

"You know, you can turn around now. It will be impossible later. If you feel you do not have the strength to carry out this mission, it is best you leave. Nothing will happen to you. We will continue without you."

Shame shot through Salah's body, piercing and electric. "I can do it. I am a soldier," Salah said, lifting his chin. He would not be remembered for weakness.

"That's good, brother." Ibrahim raised his hand. Salah clasped it, their thumbs interlocking. "Let's pray." Salah focused on Ibrahim's droning monotone. The prayer was calming.

"I have the packs. They are in the back," Ibrahim said when the prayer was over. He glanced around the parking lot. There was no one about. The four men got out of the car and walked around to the back. Inside the trunk, three backpacks and a jacket sat carefully stored in a well in the floor.

"These two are for you," Ibrahim said to Abdel and Jawad. They reached in, picking a backpack each and carefully putting it over their shoulders. Salah hung back as Ibrahim lifted the final pack. He held a strap for Salah to put his arm through, and when he did so, Ibrahim draped the backpack over Salah's shoulder with a thin smile.

Ibrahim handed each man a lanyard, their security pass, and for Salah, he held out the jacket. On the chest and the sleeve was a logo representing the firm that handled security for the Rogers Arena. "Fold this as I showed you earlier, lining outside, badge inside. Hold it in your arm." Ibrahim turned to Abdel and Jawad. "Your belts and jackets are in your backpack. Don't put them on until you are inside the building. Everything should be just as we rehearsed." Ibrahim's phone rang. He answered it and listened to the voice on the other end before wordlessly disconnecting the call.

"What is it, Ibrahim?" Jawad said.

"The others are not coming. It is nothing. The glory will be all yours. You must go. You know what to do. Paradise awaits, my brothers. *Allahu akbar.*"

"*Allahu akbar,*" the three younger men replied.

Salah swayed as the SkyTrain smoothly navigated the tracks. He was looking out over the city. He had never lived anywhere else. In the late afternoon sunshine, Vancouver was busy but not crowded. Trees and parkland accompanied much of his ride. He looked down at children playing, people walking their dogs, and the designated graffiti wall he'd hung around during his early high school years. Soon everyone would be inside watching the game.

The train was filling up rapidly. The carriage was a blur of blue, green, and white. One big guy had half his face painted blue, the other half green. A white stripe ran down the middle.

Many ethnicities were represented in the faces of his fellow passengers. At school, Salah had been good at languages, and in the carriage, he could hear people speaking French and German and what he suspected was Mandarin. He could see no one he suspected as Muslim.

In the next carriage, Salah could see the back of Abdel's head bobbing as the train sped along the track. Every few minutes the train stopped at another station. Passengers got on, but almost no one got off. Salah looked above the door at the map of the Expo line before looking out of the window once more.

The scenery changed now. The train had reached the city center. Billboards, tech company buildings, and luxury car showrooms replaced the homes and parks of earlier. The SkyTrain kept on, unconcerned by the hopes, motivations, stories, and plans of its passengers.

"The next station is Stadium-Chinatown," a female voice announced from a speaker somewhere above Salah's head. The train came to a stop and the doors slid open. Salah stepped onto the platform and looked to his left to see Abdel doing the same. Up ahead of him was Jawad. They were on their own now.

The crowd was heavy and soon swallowed Salah up. Abdel overtook him, and Salah quickened his pace to keep him in his sights. Jawad had disappeared from view. Salah looked around. He knew exactly what to do. The execution of their plan had been drilled into them over hours of meetings, rehearsals, and dummy runs. Salah had gone over the drills so many times that he roamed the layout of the arena in his sleep.

He also knew what was in his pack: cartridges filled with nails, screws, ball bearings and bolts, and most importantly, TATP, triacetone triperoxide, the terrorist's explosive of choice. It was a volatile mixture of hydrogen peroxide, acetone, and hydrochloric acid, but all they needed to make it were nail polish and bleach. Salah had bought them from his local drugstore.

TATP exploded with only slight provocation and Salah was careful to position himself among the crowd so that he couldn't be bumped. Fuses linked the bombs so they exploded simultaneously when detonated by the switch in one of his pack's pockets.

Salah regarded the hockey fans around him. They were oblivious to the fate ahead of them. They were distracted, excited about the upcoming game, anticipating a win for the home team, and possibly the cup. They had no idea how their day would end: the pain, the terror, the destruction. Nor did they know how frantic, desolate, and stunned their loved ones would be and how, by then, it would be Salah the oblivious one.

As he rounded the corner to the stadium, Salah saw Jawad and Abdel meet up and quietly go through a service entrance. From there, they'd pick up a large trash container. Using it as cover, they would get themselves in position.

As Salah walked, he attempted to shrug on his jacket as he'd been taught. He put his left arm into the sleeve and moved the backpack carefully to his other shoulder. A woman of about twenty walked past him laughing, the arm of the man next to her hanging around her neck.

Damn! Salah's second arm caught inside the sleeve, and the fabric twisted around his wrist. The more Salah struggled, the tighter the coil of fabric became, trapping him like a Chinese finger trap. He paused wrestling with his jacket to carefully remove his pack and set it on a bench. Rethreading his arm into the sleeve, Salah looked down to zip up the jacket. It was then that he caught sight of two small feet dangling over the side of the bench. Salah froze.

"No!" he hissed. His arm shot out. "Don't touch that," he said, more calmly as the boy let go of the pack he'd used to pull himself up onto the bench.

"I've lost my daddy," the boy said. His blue eyes stared out from under his bangs. "Mommy told me if I lost him, to find a policeman." Dean eyed the badge on Salah's arm, his forehead wrinkling. "Are you a policeman?"

CHAPTER TWENTY-SEVEN

S ALAH STARED AT the boy. He knew he could turn away, but his mind raced. His arrival at the stadium coincided with the busiest period for security personnel before a game. Passing through the staff check-in was the riskiest part of the whole plan. Being forced through a metal detector or submitting his bag for examination would blow the mission entirely. But close to game time, security staff were diverted to the front of house to expedite the bag checks of the last-minute crowd.

Salah was banking on the staff check-in being empty. But what if it weren't? He thought back to the doubt in Ibrahim's eyes when he'd looked at Salah in the back of the car earlier. Salah looked again at the boy.

"What's your name?"

"Dean Johnson Beresford!" Dean said. He knew his address and phone number too. He'd been practicing at school.

Salah carefully hoisted his pack onto his shoulder. "Okay, Dean. Come with me, okay?" Salah held his hand out, and wordlessly Dean slipped off the bench and took it.

Salah's energy was amped, adrenaline coursing through him. He focused on his breathing, deep breaths in and out, counting to four, as he'd been taught. Forcing himself to walk slowly, Salah matched Dean's pace, and together they made the last few hundred yards to the building that looked like a spaceship.

"Where are we going?" Dean asked.

"We'll go inside the building and find the person who looks after lost kids."

"Will my dad be there?" Salah didn't answer.

Dean tugged on his hand. "Will my dad be there?" he repeated.

"Wha—? Yeah, they'll find him for you. They'll put out an announcement for him or something. Come on, we need to walk a bit faster."

Salah was walking ahead of Dean now. The boy was hanging on his hand. Salah gripped tighter, pulling him along. He focused on the service door. He knew that behind it was a corridor. On the left, there would be a locker room for stadium staff. On the other side of that was the staff check-in. Dean was babbling. Something about his dad and Star Wars.

"Come on!" Salah said through gritted teeth. Dean's head was down and he started to grizzle. "Sorry, sorry. We'll find your dad, no problem."

Salah bent down. In one swooping movement, he lifted the boy onto his hip. Dean wasn't large for his age, but his knee hit Salah's pack. Salah froze. He closed his eyes. For a split second, he considered leaving Dean where he was but almost immediately re-committed to the idea that Dean was insurance and good cover.

"We need to get inside the building to find the nice

people who will find your dad. Just hang on a bit longer. It'll be okay." Dean nodded and rubbed his eyes.

Salah pulled open the wide glass door to the building and turned left to walk down the corridor. It was empty. He held Dean tight so that he didn't swing or move. He could see the non-descript gray door that led into the locker room, the corridor arcing away from him as it followed the cylindrical shape of the building. As he reached the door, he put his hand out to grip the handle.

"Salah!"

A chill slaked through Salah's body. He looked over and around the curve of the hallway. There stood a large, rolling waste container. In front of it were Abdel and Jawad, their eyes wide. Abdel took two steps toward him, his arm out, palm down.

"There's someone in there. At the security desk. You can't go inside. It's off. The plan is off. Abort, abort." Abdel was whisper-shouting, his curls shaking as he shook his head, his brown eyes big and beseeching.

Salah stared at Abdel, then at Jawad uncomprehendingly. They had gone over the plan a hundred times. It was inconceivable that they would abandon it now. As Abdel's words penetrated, the myriad injustices that Salah felt dictated the tune that his life danced to swirled about his mind—the racism, the bullying, his father's cancer, his mother's three jobs, their family's poverty, his poor job prospects. He thought about the prospect of salvation, honor, pride, Paradise. To him, it all seemed a wash.

But then his gaze returned to Abdel. His aggressive swagger and sneering contempt had disappeared. Salah remembered Abdel's snide remarks, the put-downs, the sense of being weak, juvenile, and unsophisticated. There was no sign of that Abdel now. Dean's foot nudged Salah's hip. His gaze hardened as he looked back at the two men who had committed to sacrificing their lives for the cause and who had ridiculed him for hesitating. Salah turned his back on them, pushed the door open, and made his way to the locker room.

Gray cabinets lined the walls. The doors of two of them hung open, keys slotted in the locks. They were empty. A trash bag lay on the beige tiled floor, and a scratched wooden chair sat next to the frosted glass window to one side. Coat hangers hung from hooks on the wall next to an alcove at the other end of the room. The walls were steel gray. They coordinated with the lockers in a way that suggested a decorator with a flair for the institutional had been hired.

To the left was another alcove and a door. Salah knew the door led to the staff check-in area and the stadium proper. He paused as he prepared himself. He could hear low voices talking on the other side of the door. Hefting Dean to position him higher on his hip, he gripped the boy tightly and focused on the door until he felt two fat, overly warm, small hands press against his cheeks, smooshing his lips together. Dean turned Salah's face to him and Salah found his brown eyes staring into Dean's blue ones.

"I want my daddy."

"I know. Nearly there, eh? I'm taking you to the nice lady who will look after you until your dad comes to get you, okay?"

Long lashes framed Dean's big blue eyes. Each eyelash was fair at the tip. Salah hadn't noticed them until now. They were almost as long as his own. The boy gave an impatient huff, but he let go of Salah's face and looked at the door. Salah grabbed the knob and opened it, his heart slamming against his chest. He walked steadily into the room.

Two men stood, each beside a machine. They were almost identical—in their mid-fifties, graying hair, both stout, with bellies protruding over their pant belts. One of them hooked his thumbs into the back of his waistband and hoisted his trousers up. Around their waists hung handcuffs, a baton, and Tasers. Radios were pinned to their lapels, wires coiling up their necks to earpieces.

Salah nodded to the men. One of them swigged from a water bottle. He stood next to the x-ray machine, his gold badge revealing his name to be "Williams." He was silent, except for when he let out a loud burp. The other guard, standing further back, grunted. The opening into the corridor that fed access to the seating area of the stadium was behind them. The walls of the corridor were glass, and Salah could see that most of the seats in the stadium were full, the ice pristine for just a few more minutes before the players' skates would slice it up.

Salah walked up to the reader mounted on the wall. He swiped his card, and as he did so, he lifted Dean an inch and dipped his head toward him, looking over at the two men. "Lost his dad."

Neither guard said anything. Salah's breathing was shallow, and he could feel sweat dripping down his back. The light on the badge reader turned red.

Salah concentrated on his breathing and tried again. This time, the green light came on. Salah quickly moved off. He took the most direct route to the corridor—between the X-ray machine and the wall. He avoided the body scanner altogether.

Salah felt the eyes of the two men on him, but they

didn't speak. Six steps, and he would be in. Five, four, three, two . . .

"Wait."

Salah stopped and turned. "Hmm?"

"You want to go that way," the burping security guard said. He pointed to his right. "Fan Services. Angie. She's great with lost kids. Tell her Don sent you."

CHAPTER TWENTY-EIGHT

DEAN COULDN'T HAVE gone far. Malcolm stood in place and swiveled, then ventured from his spot a few paces. He looked up and down the main concourse to the arena, but all he could see were people, masses of people, excitedly pounding the pavement to get to the game before it began. Among the crowd there were children, some around Dean's age and with his coloring. Several times, Malcolm's heart leaped, only for it to plunge when he realized the clothes were all wrong or he caught a glance of a face that wasn't his son's.

Malcolm ventured further into the current of the crowd. It was gathering speed, and there were fewer and fewer spaces between the people. Up ahead the mass was dense, tightly packed as fans waited their turn to pass into the stadium.

Malcolm allowed himself to be swept along by the crowd. He worried he may be leaving Dean behind, but he was equally anxious that his son had moved on ahead. Malcolm's heart hammered. The crowd pressed against him. He was unable to see further than a few people in front. The adrenaline that had slowly been building mounted in a surge. He was beginning to panic. It was hard to breathe. "Dean! Dean?" Malcolm shouted.

He pushed his way out of the heaving mass, eliciting frustrated moans from the people around him as he jostled and elbowed his way through. "Sorry. Sorry, mate. Excuse me. Thanks. Dean! Dean!" Malcolm found himself outside the throng again. He looked around, but there was still no sight of his son. He plunged back into the tide of people once more.

Close to the entrance, Malcolm was forced to come to a halt. The security point was a bottleneck, and the crowd had backed up. Again, he pushed his way through the teeming mass, this time to the front where security was checking bags and passing people through the scanner.

"I'm looking for my son. I've lost my son. Have you seen him?"

The security guard was focused, intent on his job. The man continued to delve into the purse of the woman standing in front of him, moving around its contents and peering inside. He patted the outside of her bag with both hands and zipped it up.

"Please," Malcolm tried again. "I've lost my son. Have you seen him? He's six—"

The guard looked young, in his twenties but already balding. A ring of fair hair orbited his head. He slowly looked up at Malcolm, seeming to see him for the first time. As Malcolm bit his lip, his body rigid, the guard flicked a casual hand over to the female security guard on the other side of the aisle.

Malcolm rushed over. He barged in between the woman and the person whose bag she was surveying. "I need to find my son. He's six. I've lost him."

The woman was stocky, young, and stood ramrod straight, her uniform tight across her chest, her brown hair tied back. She carried a flat, black wand in her hand. She pointed it ahead of her. "Fan Services. Up the stairs, on your right. Third floor." Malcolm started to run. "Push your way to the front if there's a crowd. What's his name?" she called out.

Malcolm skidded to a stop. "Dean."

"Six, you say?" Malcolm nodded. "Alright, I'll keep an eye out."

Peter and Diana arrived first. The armored vehicles carrying the SWAT and counter-terrorism teams were behind and would position themselves at a distance from the stadium entrance. They were not to alert the bombers or the crowd to their presence. On command, they would form a "ring of steel" around the arena, large enough, and tight enough to unleash man- and firepower sufficient to cover just about any threat.

Suicide bombers, the most challenging of menaces, were the exception. Their ability to kill tens, hundreds, thousands inside a densely packed area exacerbated their willingness to play a zero-sum game. They die, they win. They had nothing to lose.

Peter watched as undercover agents infiltrated the crowd waiting to get into the stadium, their job to identify threats within it. More would move inside to mingle with the 19,000 spectators that were rinkside.

"We're ready to lock down the outside of the building," Stockton, the SWAT team commander, told Peter.

"Let the crowd through. I don't want to alert the marks

if they've already breached. Double down on security checks. Make sure no one gets through that shouldn't," Peter responded.

Stockton whirled around. "Hopkinson, my men are trained for this. You don't have the experience—" Diana walked up, interrupting the two men.

"Commander, please meet Major Peter Hopkinson, currently on active duty, formerly of special forces specializing in infiltration and extraction, and the only person ever to receive the Canadian Victoria Cross."

Stockton's eyes widened. "You never said," he breathed.

"There was no reason to," Peter said briskly.

"Then sir, I'll stand aside and order my men on your command," Stockton replied.

"Get marksmen on the roof. Work the crowd inside. We'll survey the security cameras and look for suspicious activity."

"Shall we delay the game?"

"No, carry on as normal."

"Yes, sir." Stockton made to run to instruct his men.

"Are you sure that's the right thing?" Diana asked. "Procedure is to lock down the outside and evacuate the crowd."

"Yeah, and all that does is cover the backs of those in charge if it goes bad. If we alert the terrorists to the fact we know they're here, they'll just pull their triggers. This way, we stand a chance of getting to them before they realize the game's up."

"But more people risk being killed. If it goes bad, you'll be handed the responsibility for their deaths."

"I know that. Our choices are terrible and worse. This, in my view, is the marginally better option. The bombers have nothing to lose, remember."

Diana was surprised at what Peter was saying, but she

couldn't argue with it. They were in a no-win situation. As she listened to him, two men wearing reflective vests over their clothes came out of the arena building pushing a large waste skip. They glanced around, sizing up their environment. As the two men bent over to push the cart, their vests creased and bulged unnaturally. Diana noticed their gaits, the way they moved cautiously. They seemed to be taking cover behind the skip even as they moved.

"Over there," she whispered.

Peter turned to look. "Bingo. It's them."

CHAPTER TWENTY-NINE

"**S**HALL WE SHOOT them from behind?" Diana said. Peter blew down his nose, his lips forming a small smile at Diana's suggestion. She didn't mess around, that was for sure.

"No, it's too risky, and they'll blow themselves up if they see us coming. There are too many people around for that."

"We can jump them."

Peter nodded. "They're slipping away from the crowd, moving toward the refuse area. Let's get them when they go around the back. We can do it quietly. No one will even notice. I'll take the guy on the left, you the one on the right. They both look right-handed."

"I can't see their detonators," Diana replied. She could see the bomber's hands flat against the waste cart as they pushed it.

"They'll reach for them. That's our priority."

"Alive?"

"I should say so. They'll take us with them, if not. Quick, smooth, and efficient, okay? The explosives they're carrying are volatile," Peter said.

Matching each other's movements so precisely that they acted as a single unit, Diana and Peter crept up behind the two men without making a sound. In a noiseless, coordinated attack, they each wrapped a choking arm around the men's necks and forced their right hands behind their backs. Forcing the men over, Diana and Peter immediately followed up by grabbing their left hands and pushing them to the floor with a knee to the spine. It was clinical and barely violent. The men were disabled in less than three seconds. Neither bomber had the time or the presence of mind to resist.

Diana rolled up Jawad's sleeve and found his detonator switch just above the elasticated cuff of his sweatshirt. "Got it."

"Mine too."

Diana spoke into her radio. "Armed response and bomb squad needed stat. Defuse explosives."

A couple of curious fans milled around gawking, and a tall twig of a man readied his phone for a selfie. Peter, with a knee still in Abdel's back and an elbow forcing his head into the concrete, roared, "Move!" and the startled fan took off at a sprint. Within seconds, two SWAT teams cleared the area of stragglers and took up position two hundred yards away. Diana and Peter waited, unmoving and barely breathing, their bodies fixing Abdel and Jawad to the ground.

Sweat was pouring down Diana's face, but she held fast to Jawad. He had four inches and many pounds on her. She was thankful for the hours of training she had put in, both on her own and with Peter. They had practiced their moves repeatedly, anticipating as many scenarios as they could imagine until their actions were seamless. Still, she would be glad when the bomb squad arrived to put them all out of their misery.

After what seemed like an age, a small, slight figure clad head to foot in explosive protection gear casually walked over to them "Good evening, all," a jovial female voice said, muffled by the large, cube-shaped helmet covering her head. "Captain Lisa Anderson, Bomb Squad. What have you got for me?"

"Switches in their sleeves, bombs around their waists, maybe elsewhere," Peter replied.

"Gotcha. Give me a moment to get set up," Captain Anderson said. "Hold tight," she added unnecessarily.

Click. Click. Click.

Wire by wire, Anderson went slowly, minimizing her movements and treating their charges as tenderly as newborns. That she was able to do so relied solely on the effort Peter put into pushing Abdel's body into the concrete. Veins popped in his arms and his temple as he pinned the bomber down in a vice-like grip.

Carefully, the bomb disposal officer broke the circuit between the explosives and the detonator, and the bombs from each other. Then, with Peter's help, she gently removed the explosives from Abdel's body and placed them on the ground a few feet away.

"Go," Peter ordered Abdel when she was done. Abdel, who had not resisted their efforts, looked at him vacantly. Peter indicated the men carrying semi-automatic weapons two hundred yards away. "Go!" Peter leveled a boot on Abdel's backside and gave him a shove. The now-impotent Abdel started to walk slowly, his hands up, toward the perimeter of the ring as two SWAT team members, guns raised, started forward to meet him.

Click. Click. Click. Captain Anderson coolly repeated her process with Jawad. Diana and Peter held their breaths as Peter helped Diana pin Jawad down, their hearts pounding in their ears.

"Okay, all disconnected," Anderson said cheerfully as she stood up straight after cutting the final connection. She lifted the explosives from Jawad's body and placed them on the ground next to the others.

Peter let out an audible sigh and pulled Jawad to standing. He pushed him, too, in the direction of the ring perimeter, "Move."

Jawad stumbled, then started to walk, his arms aloft. He quickly disappeared into the scrum of SWAT team members who swirled up to surround him. Diana and Peter stood quietly, breathing deeply until their heart rates returned to normal.

"You should get out of here. Clear the area now. My team will dispose of these explosives. We brought robots with us." Lisa Anderson gathered up her equipment.

"Okay, we're going," Peter said, unreasonably annoyed at being told what to do.

"Thanks," Diana added more generously. "You were fantastic. We couldn't have done it without you."

"Yeah, thanks," Peter conceded gruffly.

As they walked from the area, Diana rubbed her face. "What now? We can't be sure it's all dealt with."

"Nope, we have to continue as planned." Peter saw Stockton coming toward them.

"We've got the prisoners in custody, sir."

"Let me interrogate them," Diana said to Peter. "You go into the stadium and search the crowd."

"I'll show you to their location, ma'am," Stockton said.

"Good luck," Peter said. "Don't take any guff from them and don't do anything I wouldn't do."

Diana dipped her chin and looked at him. "As if."

Diana looked at the man on the bench opposite her. They were in an Emergency Task Force van. The door was closed. There were no windows. The rank aroma of previous inhabitants hung in the air. The space was hot, airless, and unpleasant. And none of that mattered.

Abdel looked at her, contempt now reasserting itself. Throughout all his training, his praying, his radicalization, he'd had an unswerving conviction that he would be successful. He would complete Allah's work and enter Paradise. To be here in this hot, stuffy, and stinky van offended him. And being in thrall to *a woman* added further insult to his outrage.

He looked at her with his head tilted back, his arms folded. Diana ignored his seething gaze. She was concerned about this interview. A quick background check had produced nothing that gave her anything to work with. Abdel had no connections that were of any importance to him. He was divorced from a wife who had a restraining order against him. He was estranged from his parents. He worked only odd jobs here and there. He had no children.

"My name is Diana. I am a consultant for the Vancouver Police Department." Abdel was unmoved. "How are you feeling?" He shrugged.

"Can I get you a water? Coffee?" Still nothing. "Well, if you don't mind, I'm going to have a drink. It's hot in here."

Diana reached down and picked up one of the two bottles of water she had brought into the van with her. She drank greedily from it. A trickle of water spilled from the side of her mouth. She wiped it with the back of her hand, exhaling deeply.

"You gave us the runaround out there. Thirsty work."

She kept ahold of the bottle in one hand, the cap in the other. The van shifted gently as someone leaned against it. "Is anyone waiting for you, Abdel? Is there anyone we can call?" Abdel's eyes flickered. There was someone.

"A girlfriend? A brother?" No response. "Well, you just let us know when you're ready."

Diana looked around the van, lifted her shoulders high, and dropped them. She pressed her lips together and looked at Abdel innocently. "Are you sure you don't want some water? You're sweating." Abdel still didn't respond. *Wait it out.*

Diana regarded Abdel's direct gaze, the slouch as he sat, the not-so-faint stench of contempt emanating from him. Like Chakrib earlier. The scene in that disused building seemed like a long time ago now.

Diana looked at her watch. "It's gone five o'clock. My dog will be waiting for me." Another flicker. "His name is Max. He's a Maltese terrier. Here, would you like to see a picture of him?"

Diana fished in the side pocket of her cargo pants and pulled out a laminated picture of Max sitting on a red tartan cushion. He looked adorable. Diana held it out for Abdel. She waited a few seconds. Abdel's eyes flicked over the image, but he showed no further interest, and with a theatrical sigh, Diana took the picture back.

"Okay, well, it's past time for his walk. I need to go." Diana knocked on the door to let the team outside know she was coming out. She bent to stand in the confined space.

"Marley."

"Eh?"

"Marley. That's my dog's name. After the movie, you know?"

CHAPTER THIRTY

"WHAT IS HE, Marley?"

"Boston terrier mostly. A bit of bulldog in there too, probably. He was a rescue."

"What's he look like?"

"Small, obviously. Dark gray, big ears with a pug face. Bouncy."

Diana laughed. "Yes, I can relate to the bounciness of terriers."

Abdel gave a wry smile. "He loves everyone. Terrible watchdog."

"Where's Marley now, Abdel?"

"At a friend's."

"What was your plan for him? After this." Diana waved her hand in a flat circle to encompass the entire van.

"My friend would keep him when I didn't come back. He has three of his own. I knew he would be alright with Marley. And Marley with him."

"Did anyone else in your group have dogs they were going to leave behind?"

"Dunno. You'd have to ask them." Abdel's eyelids lowered. He'd said enough.

"Here, are you sure you don't want any water?" Diana held out the unopened bottle at her feet. Abdel hesitated for a moment, then reached out and took it from her. He drank half the contents in one long pull.

"So there were more than the two of you?" Silence. "Abdel?" Diana prompted. She looked at her watch. "You know, I really must be going to see to Max. He'll be going ape and dying to get out. I'll come back later."

Again, she bent to push herself to a standing position. Abdel spoke so quietly she almost didn't hear him.

"There were three of us. Salah's inside. He had a kid with him."

Peter listened in silence as Diana reeled off the information she'd gathered. "Salah Abaaoud. Nineteen. Five feet ten inches. Stubbly beard. Wearing a security uniform. Has a child with him, a kid he somehow picked up on the way in. A spectator has reported his child missing. A boy. Six. Name of Dean Beresford. We think it could be him. Our target used the child to bypass security procedures. Abaaoud has a backpack."

"Okay, got it. The pack will be filled with explosives and connected to a switch like the others. Tell them not to put out announcements about the lost child. We don't need members of the public intercepting them if they are still together," Peter said. He broke the call and turned to the room.

"Listen up everyone! We're looking for a man *with a six-year-old boy*!"

Peter relayed the descriptions of the pair to the team operating the security cameras. Normally five strong, an additional ten had been hastily recruited. All fifteen of them were now leaning forward in their chairs, staring intently at their screens, manipulating camera views as they searched the crowd. Their team leader and Peter stood behind them, staring above their heads.

Against the front wall, high above them, a bank of large screens magnified the views from the spectator area. Normally, one would focus on the rink, the game playing ostensibly in the background, a perk for those security team members not assigned to crowd management. Today, however, every camera was turned away from the ice and now faced the crowd, whirring quietly as the camera operators maneuvered them across the heads of the spectators as they searched for a fake security guard and a six-year-old boy.

Peter was in battle mode. He had shut down all peripheral thoughts and feelings unnecessary to the task at hand. He stared at the screens, flicking from one to another to another, hyper-focused, providing an extra pair of eyes surveying the stadium arena, occasionally instructing a camera operator with one-word orders. Diana quietly appeared next to him, breathless from her run from the police command unit. He barely registered her presence.

A shout went up. The central screen in the bank above them switched views. In the new shot, there was a mass of faces looking out over the rink. A few were holding foam fingers. Nearly all of them were wearing the home team's colors. The Canucks were already down 0-1, and agony, hope, and fear were etched across the spectator's faces. Little did they know the real, physical danger in their midst. Behind them, standing in the rear walkway looking out at the rink was Salah. He was still carrying Dean.

"Stay here." Peter was speaking to Diana. He hadn't taken his eyes off the screen. She had never seen him like this.

"What are you going to do?"

He did look at her then. "What I can." Peter leaned over the shoulder of a camera operator. "How do I get there?" He pointed at the screen. Just under the stadium roof, there was a platform. Mounted on it were speakers and lighting equipment. A Canadian flag hung from the ceiling.

The camera operator swiveled in her seat and pointed to a door at the top of a flight of metal stairs in the corner of the room. "Follow the service corridor all the way. It will open up to the arena and run around above the top level. You can climb up from there.

"How much higher will I be than this guy?" Peter pointed at the screen where Salah stood.

"Based on where he is now, about twenty feet. But you'll be on the opposite side of the arena."

"Perfect."

Peter turned and made his way to the door that led to the uppermost courseway. He walked up to Stockton who was standing at the back of the room awaiting orders. Peter held out his hands. Stockton shot him a steady gaze and mutely passed his rifle to Peter. Without another word, he looked back at Diana. She nodded and watched as he climbed the stairs two steps at a time and passed through the door into the corridor beyond.

Peter crouched on the platform beneath the stadium roof, resting his rifle on a speaker. He looked down the gun's scope at the scene before him.

Salah stood behind a wall above the highest bank of seats in the arena. He faced the ice, but his eyes, overly bright, flicked around, his mind not on the game. On either side of him were spectators who stood, drinks in hand, transfixed by the sport playing out before them. Salah twisted to allow a heavy-set man to pass. As he did so, Peter caught sight of the pack draped over Salah's right shoulder.

Dean's fair hair glittered in the shade of the upper spectator area, his blond highlights picked out by the random LED lights. He was holding something. Peter adjusted his scope to see what it was. Dean held a trading card in his hand.

Peter needed a clear sight, but Salah had Dean on his hip still. The youngster obscured Peter's view. The boy wriggled in Salah's grasp and Salah turned, alerted by something to his right. Peter followed his gaze. Diana stood there. She had her hand on Salah's arm. *What the hell?*

Diana faced Salah, smiling. Her hair was pulled into a ponytail, strands falling around her face. An angry roar went up. The crowd stood en masse to dispute the referee's latest decision, obscuring the group on the walkway from Peter's sight. When they settled back down, Diana was speaking to Salah, her arms outstretched, nodding, smiling, her eyes glowing. *Diana was offering to take the boy. She was trying to help him. Dear God, why did she do these things?*

Dean leaned forward, but Salah pressed his hand against the boy's chest, a shake of his head communicating his refusal. His right hand was deep in his pocket. Peter knew that in the seconds it would take for his shot to travel, the scene could change. He considered his options.

Diana was closer to Salah and Dean now. She was coaxing the tearful boy, her arms still outstretched, a hand cupping his face. She looked directly into Dean's eyes. The eyes of the boy in the bunker in the middle of the desert floated into Peter's mind, followed by the image of the man who had raced back to save them, and the terrible choice Peter had faced. Here was a different boy, a different man, another tough choice. And he still had no clear shot.

Salah's eyes widened. A commotion erupted. A man was rushing the crowd on the walkway. Diana half turned but collapsed face-first as Salah pushed her against a wall. The boy in his arms leaned forward, reaching out to the man who lunged toward them, the bomber's right hand rising to the ceiling. This was the moment.

Peter inhaled. He squeezed the trigger, his eyes unblinking. The sound of the crowd roared in his ears. Peter waited and watched helplessly as the scene unfurled before him. 3 . . . 2 . . .

Salah convulsed. Red spray erupted in a puff behind him. He crumpled. Dean instinctively turned from the bullet as it striated Salah's skull. The boy, spattered with blood, fell from Salah's arms. Diana threw herself backward, crashing to the floor, positioning herself to cushion the explosives as Salah's body collapsed onto hers.

A small box flew through the air. It climbed, spinning, the light catching as it turned on its axis before changing course and descending, gaining speed as it hurtled to earth. Peter crouched, frozen in place as seconds passed and time slowed to a crawl, the crowd still roaring around him, oblivious to the danger in their midst. On the concourse, Diana scrambled to push Salah's body off hers and she kneeled, looking up, shielding her eyes, searching, unseeing, the floodlights blinding her.

Then, there! Diana caught sight of the switch. It was barreling toward her. She waited, watching, following its trajectory. The switch dropped smartly and Diana's hand closed around it. There was no flash, no smoke, no sound, no wind. Peter finally exhaled.

Carefully, he pushed on his gun's safety and pulled back from the sight, lowering the rifle, his mind blank. He stepped down from the platform and prepared to return the way he had come.

Malcolm rushed forward and swept up his son. He cradled him gently, desperately. They huddled against the wall. Dean was scared but unharmed and he wanted his mama. For Malcolm, that reunion couldn't come a moment too soon.

CHAPTER THIRTY-ONE

"**C**AN'T I DRIVE for once?" Diana said.

"Nope," Peter replied. "You're not registered. You're a consultant, remember, not a
member of VPD proper."

"Funny how I can lay my life on the line for VPD but
not drive one of their cars."

"Yep, one of the great mysteries of life." Diana walked
around to the passenger side of the car. "They haven't
found Kloch yet," Peter said.

"Huh, interesting. I wonder where he's got to."

"He's probably run for the hills now that his mate,
Greene, is in the clink."

Diana and Peter made the ride in silence. They were
tired. It had been an eventful few days. Diana closed her
eyes.

"We're here," Peter said when he pulled up outside her
apartment building.

"Already?" Diana asked, looking around in surprise.
"That was fast. More grandpa than granny this time." Diana
often complained that Peter drove too slowly.

"Now you're just being sexist."

Diana chuckled. "Speak tomorrow. I might go into the office for a bit if I'm not needed."

"Why do you keep working for that magazine? Why don't you come work for VPD full-time?"

Diana sighed. "Donaldson did offer me the hours, but I'm not ready to give up writing just yet."

"You spend more time with us than at the magazine, you know. And what you do for them hardly compares to what you do for us."

"I know. I'll give it more thought now that this crisis is over." Diana opened the passenger door. "Thanks for the lift. I appreciate it."

"Any time."

Diana leaned over and kissed Peter on the cheek before getting out of the car. "Good work today," she whispered.

"Thank you. You too."

Diana sat back and looked at Peter curiously. He'd been efficient but distant since the shooting. "Are you okay?"

"Yes, yes, I'm fine. I just need to go home and get a good night's sleep." Peter turned to her and gave her a tired smile.

"Yeah, me too." Diana reached out and squeezed his hand before opening the door and getting out. It was a warm night. She didn't like the idea of Peter going home to an empty apartment. Not after what he'd done.

"Sure you don't want to come in?" she tried.

"I'm sure. Thanks for asking. You have a nice night."

After the day they'd had, this seemed an unsatisfactory, perfunctory parting, but Diana didn't say more. She got her bag out of the trunk, and made her way into her apartment building, pausing at the entrance to wave to Peter, who was still waiting by the curb. Was he making sure she got in safely? She shook her head and smiled again.

"Ms. Hunter." Larry, the doorman, greeted her enthusiastically the moment she set foot in the lobby. "Good evening, did you have a good day?"

"Busy, Larry, busy," Diana replied. "How's things?"

"Everything's been quiet here. Ms. Jenkins is upstairs."

"Thank you, Larry," Diana said with an appreciative smile. "I'll see you later."

"Of course, Ms. Hunter."

A minute or two later, Diana unlocked her front door to Max's excited yipping and barking. As soon as she was inside, Max jumped on her, doing his best to climb up her leg in excitement.

"How's my wonderful boy?" Diana cooed, dropping her bag to the floor. She kneeled and picked up her ball of fluff. He happily proceeded to lick her entire face.

"He's been going crazy for the past half-hour," Terri said with a chuckle. "I swear he's psychic."

Diana laughed. "I don't know about psychic, but he's Mommy's smart boy, isn't he?" She scratched between Max's ears, but that didn't deter him from his goal, which seemed to be to lick her from head to toe. "Everything okay?" she asked Terri.

The girl nodded. "Everything's been peaceful. I haven't gotten this much studying done in months."

"That's great," Diana replied. "Because I've got a proposition for you. But first, I need a shower, a glass of wine, and something to eat."

Fifteen minutes later, Diana was in the kitchen, sipping a nice red wine while Terri threw together some dinner for them.

"So, you were saying something about a proposition?" Terri asked as she chopped vegetables for a salad. Two steaks were sizzling in a pan. The meaty smell made Diana's stomach rumble.

"I'm joining VPD full-time," Diana began.

"You're going to leave the magazine?" Terri asked in surprise.

Diana shrugged. "It's time. I'm tired of dealing with all the administrative work that comes with it."

When Diana joined *Crime & Punishment*, she had hoped the position would offer her access to resources that would make the investigation into her parents' deaths easier. But working with VPD was more valuable for that, and all around more beneficial.

"But I thought you loved to write," Terri said.

"I do, but I don't do much writing anymore. Anyway, working for VPD is a lot more fun."

Terri cocked an eyebrow and grinned. "Only you would find spending the day intercepting suicide bombers 'fun.'" She saw Diana's mouth fall open. "Just guessing," Terri added quickly.

"Hey, I'm wired differently," Diana said. "It'll mean odd hours and being away from home a lot so I was wondering if you'd be interested in more work? Regular hours. If you're here, I won't have to worry about Max. And maybe you can help out with a few chores like picking up groceries, a bit of cleaning, and stuff like that. I'd pay you a salary."

Terri hadn't said much about her home life, but Diana had gleaned enough to know that things weren't all rosy for her there. Terri had a multitude of brothers, several of whom operated over on the wrong side of right while the others sounded as though they would make the jump soon. They appeared to rule the roost too, with Terri and her mother doing all the chores as well as making all the money, at least the money that came from legal sources. In an unguarded moment, Terri had told of hiding cash from her dog-sitting jobs in a box of dog treats only to have one of her brothers find it and buy a bag of cocaine with it. He'd shared it with his brothers, doing lines of it on the living room coffee table.

Terri stopped chopping, her knife frozen in mid-air. She stared at Diana, eyes wide and mouth agape. "Are you serious?" she croaked.

Diana nodded. "I don't expect you to be my maid or anything, but I figure this way you can drop your other pet-sitting clients, which will make it easier for you with school. And you'll be doing me a massive favor. Win-win."

Terri squealed and went to hug her new boss. "Whoa, put that knife down first please," Diana said, taking a half-step backward.

"That would be fantastic, thank you." Terri's eyes sparkled. "I would love that."

Later, after Terri had gone home, Diana took Max out for a walk. Terri had offered to take him, but Diana wanted a bit of fresh air to clear her mind. She did some of her best thinking when she walked Max.

As Diana took her usual route along the promenade, she got the feeling that she was being watched. When Max stopped to investigate a bush, Diana turned slowly, pretending to study the shoreline, but there was no one there. She turned back feeling uneasy. As she carried on walking Max, she continued to check, but every time, there was no one.

Diana's phone rang. "Hey Amanda, what's up?"

"No peace for the wicked. You need to get yourself down here. We have an active hostage situation. Le Caïman. The sheikh."

CHAPTER THIRTY-TWO

L E CAÏMAN WAS an upscale French restaurant and virtually an institution in Vancouver.

"He was having dinner with his son and daughter in the restaurant," Amanda told Diana over the phone.

"Damn!" Diana texted Peter. "Have they made any demands yet?"

"He wants to talk to you," Amanda replied.

"Who does?"

"Kloch."

"What? Bernard Kloch? Of Blue Panther?"

"He's on the scene."

"Kloch's taken hostages? Are you serious?"

"As a heart attack," Amanda replied.

"Why does he want to talk to me?"

"I don't know. That's all he'd say. Until you get there, he's not saying another word."

Diana switched to Peter's incoming call. "How long, Peter?"

"Ten minutes, tops," he replied. Diana switched back to Amanda.

"Okay, Amanda, we'll be there in ten. I'll let you know more when I'm on the scene."

Amanda hung up. Diana ran home to drop Max off. Back in the apartment, she grabbed her bag and went down to the lobby to await Peter.

"Hello again, Ms. Hunter," Larry said.

"Hello, Larry," she sighed.

"Going out again?"

"Yup, no peace for the wicked my boss tells me, right?"

"You don't seem terribly wicked to me, Ms. Hunter."

"It would appear that not everyone agrees with you there, Larry. Today has been quite the day." Peter's car pulled up outside. "And here I go again. 'Night, Larry."

"Kloch's taken the sheikh hostage, and the only demand he's made so far is that he must talk to me," Diana told Peter as she clambered into the car. She'd barely closed the door before Peter accelerated away.

"Any idea what he might want?"

Diana shrugged. "All I can think of is that he's heard about Greene and wants out of the country."

"The guy is a security expert. He'll have contacts all over the world. He didn't need to pull a stunt like this to get out of the country. He could have just disappeared. We'd never have found him."

"Exactly. So, what could he possibly want?"

The forecourt of Le Caïman was full of vehicles and armed Emergency Task Force personnel. They were quiet and still. Diana and Peter climbed out of their car and headed to the ETF van.

"Who's in charge?" Peter asked.

"I am," said a familiar voice. "Glad you're here, Major. And very glad to see you again, Ms. Hunter."

"Stockton," Peter said. "Thanks for the gun earlier. Very helpful. What have we got?"

"Bernard Kloch, along with five masked gunmen, have taken over Le Caïman. Shots were fired, and as far as we can determine, the sheikh's bodyguards are dead."

"Are there any other hostages?"

"About fifteen or so people, customers and staff. We think there are two other people in the sheikh's party in there with him."

"Kloch wants to talk to me. Did he say why?" Diana said.

"No, ma'am. Just said he'll only speak to you. No one else."

"Then let's get him on the phone."

Stockton waved her into the van. Inside was a mobile command station. There was a bank of three computer screens, cameras, and communication equipment. They were all against one wall. Two members of the ETF sat with headphones watching the screens that broadcast the scene outside from different angles.

"Get Kloch on the line," Stockton said as he handed Diana a headset.

"Is she there?" Kloch asked the moment he answered the call.

"I'm here, Mr. Kloch. What can I do for you?" Diana said.

"Not like this. I want you to come inside," Kloch demanded.

Diana was tempted, but one look at Peter's scowl told her she'd have a fight on her hands. "Mr. Kloch, you know I can't do that. Why don't you tell me what you want?"

"If you don't come in here, I'm going to start shooting hostages. One person every minute. I'll work my way through them and end with the sheikh himself," Kloch said. He cut the call.

"Call him again," Stockton ordered the operator. Kloch didn't pick up.

"I have to go in there," Diana said.

"You're not going anywhere," Peter growled. He'd been standing quietly in the back.

"Peter, I don't have a choice. Did you hear his voice? He's serious. He will kill those people if I don't go in." Diana's words were strong, but she said them gently. She sensed an unusual fragility beneath Peter's usual gruffness.

"There has to be another way," Peter countered, but Diana could see he knew there wasn't.

"Let's talk outside," she said.

When they were out of earshot of the van, Diana spoke quietly. "I'll be okay," she said quietly and with a small smile.

"Okay? Walking into a situation like this? Captives at gunpoint? No idea why he wants to talk to you? Unarmed? After today?" Peter kept his voice low. He looked tired. There were dark shadows under his eyes, and his voice was hoarse.

"I don't have a choice," Diana repeated. "Remember, this is the life we have. Our options are often terrible and worse."

Peter blew out his cheeks and walked away a few steps.

He wanted this day to end. Diana continued to watch him evenly. He spun around, his eyes flicked up at hers.

"You've got ten minutes, then I'm coming in after you," he said as he walked back to her.

"You?" Diana asked.

"Yes, me. You think I'd trust anyone else with your safety?"

Diana couldn't help the smile that curled her lips. If she'd had any doubts about it before, she was certain of it now. She was absolutely, head over heels in love with the blunt but very attractive Peter Hot-kinson. Unfortunately, now wasn't the best moment to dwell on it.

Stockton jumped out of the van and came over. We need a decision, Ms. Hunter."

"I'm going in, Commander. Peter will lead backup."

Stockton nodded. "Yes, ma'am."

Diana went back inside the van. "Put me through to Kloch again." The operator put through the call.

"What?" Kloch answered.

"I'll come in, but on one condition. You release the hostages first."

"No!" Kloch said. "Of course, I won't do that."

"Look, you already have the sheikh. I've said I'll come in. The additional hostages don't strengthen your hand. They are a liability. A distraction. All that moving, crying, and wailing. You don't need the distraction of fifteen other people."

"No!" Kloch yelled again.

"Then release the sheikh and his entourage. Do you want to cause an international incident?"

"I don't care about international incidents." There was a pause, and Diana could hear heavy breathing down the line.

"But you know what?" Kloch was sounding hoarse and

breathless. "You're right. I just need you and the sheikh and his family. I'll let everyone else go as soon as you're standing at the door to the restaurant. No wires. No gun. Only you. Understand?"

"Deal," Diana said quickly.

She jumped out of the van. Peter was waiting for her. "Ten minutes, okay? And then we're coming in," he said.

She smiled. "I know. Don't worry." She turned away from him, but before she could take a step, Peter grabbed her hand. She spun back to him, frowning.

He looked torn, but determination quickly replaced his indecision. He yanked her against him and in a second, he was kissing her. Diana froze, then softened and kissed him back hard. They broke apart, both of them breathing heavily.

Peter leaned his forehead against hers. "No heroics, Diana," he whispered. "I can't lose you. Remember your life is important to other people, too."

"I promise. No heroics."

"Then get going before I stop you."

CHAPTER THIRTY-THREE

D IANA DIDN'T LINGER. She turned quickly, making her way across the street, forcing herself to focus on the dangerous situation ahead. She stopped on the sidewalk in front of the door to the restaurant.

Behind and above her, twenty marksmen, on Peter's orders, trained their guns on the door to the restaurant. Fifty combat personnel were waiting down three side streets. Surrounding apartments and businesses had been evacuated. Everyone was tense, waiting, the silence only broken by the whirring of helicopters flying above.

The door opened and the hostages filed out with their hands up. Everyone looked terrified. As each person cleared the doorway, they ran toward the police vehicles. The last woman to walk out wore chef's whites. A masked man in a t-shirt and jeans, armed with an AK-47 appeared around the door and waved Diana in. She straightened her shoulders and walked inside.

As always, Le Caïman was beautiful with its airy interior, pale yellow and cream walls, and mahogany furnishings. Warm lighting, wine-red upholstered benches, and vases filled with flowers added to the normally welcoming ambiance. That was where the elegance of the situation ended, however. Three bodies lay on the floor.

Diana quickly took stock. The sheikh, Halil, and a woman with a family resemblance who looked in her early twenties sat at a table almost in the middle of the restaurant. Two masked men stood over them, along with Kloch, his face exposed. Two other masked men were stationed at the back of the room, guarding the rear entrance. The final man stood by the door, gun at the ready.

The door closed behind her, and Diana heard the lock click. Someone patted her down. "Go," a male voice ordered her.

Diana walked forward. "Your Highness," she greeted the sheikh.

"Ms. Hunter." The sheikh's voice was calm, but his eyes darted around the room. He had his arm around the shoulder of the young woman beside him.

"So, Kloch, what do you want?" Diana asked.

Kloch took off his wire-rimmed glasses and rubbed the bridge of his nose. He looked tired and scared. He was doing a good job hiding it, but he pulled at his clothes and blew out his cheeks nervously. Diana noticed that even in this fraught situation, he wore his Rolex.

"I don't have a lot of time," he said, thrusting his chin forward defiantly despite his anxiety. "I'm not a fool. I know your people will storm this restaurant in what, ten or fifteen minutes?"

"They won't breach," Diana replied.

"You're lying, but it doesn't matter. I'm a dead man anyway."

"What did you want to say to me?" Diana asked.

Kloch started to pace in front of her. "I want you to do something."

"Okay, what?"

"You think you've worked it out, but you're wrong. You think Greene is behind the bomb plot, don't you? That Greene wanted a "wag the dog" scenario." He stopped pacing to gauge Diana's reaction. When she didn't give any, he resumed.

"But that's not true. They indeed want a war, but Greene's not the main man here. He's merely the puppet they want in the Prime Minister's seat."

Kloch gesticulated wildly as he walked. Diana remained impassive. "But then you started digging around and somehow managed to find out the plan *and* foil it, and they are furious. They're blaming me."

"You're not making any sense, Kloch. What are you talking about? Who's blaming you? For what? Who is this 'they'?"

"They're blaming me for the failure of the bombing today."

"So you were responsible for that? You were behind it?"

"Yes, of course! Who else has the contacts to set up cells of suicide bombers inside Canada? The plan was to kill Al Omair at the opera, then bomb the arena, but you put an end to both and ruined everything."

Diana stared at him, nonplussed. "Then who do you work for?"

"There's a cabal, a group of bad actors who have been pulling the strings for a long time in this country and many others. They've got their fingers in every pie, from legit businesses and politics to organized crime. They have a huge amount of money and even more power."

Diana barely held back the laugh that was threatening to bubble up. "A cabal? What is this? A cheesy B-rated movie? Why do they want a war?"

Kloch shrugged. "More money, more power. Chaos that they can hide behind while making even more money and gaining even more power. These people are pathological."

"Mr. Kloch, Bernard, you know you sound crazy, right?"

"I know. But what I'm saying is the truth. I've been working for them for years. I've made a lot of money off them. There's a man who acts as their fixer. He brings me in."

"Please, Mr. Kloch, do you think me a fool?"

Kloch ignored her question. "But even he doesn't know what I know."

"Wait, stop, slow down. Explain this to me. The deal with Firat was for a Canadian to kill the sheikh. ILIF would "retaliate" with a bombing. You were organizing both, am I right? Kloch nodded. "So the deal with Firat must have been off because you didn't kill the sheikh and his son. So why did you go through with the bombing? ILIF wouldn't take responsibility. Greene was locked up. Your objectives wouldn't be met."

"You underestimate the craven nature of the people you are dealing with, Ms. Hunter. The order came down to carry out the bombing, regardless. Inciting regional instability provides these people with their bread and butter. They like to poke the bear. It creates the conditions upon which they thrive. A bit of suicide bombing in Canada would do them no harm at all."

"But who were the people you recruited to carry out the bombings?"

Kloch shrugged. "Just random delinquents. A few

words in the ears of the right people, and they're not difficult to find and program to do your bidding. But then you know all about that, don't you, Ms. Hunter?"

Diana's eyes narrowed. "And ILIF?"

Kloch continued. "ILIF wouldn't take responsibility, but another terrorist organization would have come forward to take the credit. Fanatics have huge egos, they can't help themselves."

"That wouldn't make Firat happy."

Kloch spat. "Firat? Who cares about that pussy boy?"

"Then, why are you here?" Diana looked at the sheikh. "If you weren't going to fulfill that part of the deal, why take the sheikh hostage now and kill his bodyguards?"

"Because I knew you would come."

"Me? You did this all for me? Why am I so important?"

Kloch laughed. "I'm telling you this because you need to hunt them down. The cabal. All of them. No one else can do this, only you. You are the only one who can get to the bottom of it. You have the smarts. You have the perfect motivation."

Diana frowned. "You're not making any sense, Kloch. What do you mean, only I can do this? What can only I do?"

"I've failed the cabal," Kloch said. "I'll be dead within the week, but I'm not going to go down without a fight. Putting you on their trail is my pièce de résistance. Through you, I'll get my revenge from the grave!"

Diana looked around the room at the five men with automatic weapons, the three bodies on the floor, the pale, scared faces of the sheikh and his son and daughter, and Kloch, also carrying an automatic weapon, pacing the room, arms flailing as he passionately spoke his crazy talk. Diana slowly put herself between Kloch and the sheikh, inching her way around.

"I need you on the outside, hunting them down." Kloch wasn't letting up. "They have to be eliminated. This has been going on way too long. You are the only one who can hold them accountable."

"Mr. Kloch, I don't know whether I believe there's some massive conspiracy to defraud this country beyond what you and Greene planned, but I do believe that you are the immediate threat, and that is all I care about right now."

"I know you. You'll dig to find out whether I'm telling the truth or not, especially when I tell you what I know," Kloch replied.

"Let the sheikh and his family go. Then you can tell me all about it."

Kloch raised his gun and pointed it at the sheikh. "You need to listen to me now!" Al Omair shrunk momentarily before composing himself. A resolute expression settled on his face as he prepared to face his death with courage.

"Stop!" Diana shouted. She kicked out and managed to catch Kloch in the ribs as he fired. He stumbled. The bullet hit the wall.

Kloch growled. "Grab her," he ordered his men. Diana feinted to duck the guy coming toward her, but there was another masked gunman behind him. He grabbed her arm and pulled her into a bear hug, holding her tight.

Kloch lowered his gun and stepped up to her. "Stupid woman! Do you know who this group is? What they have done? Have you any idea? All these years, on their orders, I have followed you. Watched you grow up, from clueless student to celebrated spy."

"You are lying!" Diana yelled. She struggled against the body of the man holding her. He tightened his grip.

"The cabal gave the order to kill your parents!" Kloch shouted.

Blood roared in Diana's head. "You are lying," she snarled again.

"It's true. I did the jobs myself. I killed your parents. Both of them. And I know who your real father is."

CHAPTER THIRTY-FOUR

"IT WASN'T DIFFICULT to make your mother's death look like a suicide, and when that cop father of yours got too close to the truth, I dealt with him too." Kloch was circling her now. "Remember that note on your bed? I was the one who left it." Diana glowered at him. "Don't you want to know who your real father is?" Diana blinked three times in quick succession.

"Your mother was already pregnant with you when she met John Hunter, you know." Diana took a deep breath through her nose. She was still pinned to the man behind her. "And she knew it. Did she ever tell your father? She clearly didn't tell you. Anyhow, it is of no matter. They certainly brought you up in a tight, nuclear unit. Played happy families. It was as though there was nothing unto-ward, nothing that would suggest that your mother, dear Lydia, was hiding a secret. A big secret. You don't know what it was, I know that. But I'm going to tell you now.

"Before John Hunter, Lydia was Neil Hawthorne's girl-friend. He's the fixer for the cabal, the only one who knows their identities. Your darling mother was a gangster's moll.

A high-class, big-money moll for sure, all private jets and exotic resorts, but a moll nonetheless. Hawthorne's a clever guy. It's from him that you get your brains. Did you never wonder about that?"

Kloch was telling the truth. Every gestural slip and micro-expression indicated truth, pride, and satisfaction. Diana reeled.

"You are dead," she said slowly.

"I know. A few days, no longer."

"But why? Why did you kill them?"

Kloch shrugged. "I was ordered to. They never told me why, and I never asked."

"So, you were a good little soldier. A good little *murdering* soldier."

"Of course," Kloch said with a grin. "How do you think I got to be CEO of Blue Panther?"

Diana shook her head. "You disgust me. You don't even have the balls to take responsibility for your actions. You're blaming it all on some mythical group of crazies."

Kloch gave Diana a hostile smile and marched over. He slapped her across the face. Pain exploded in her head, but she lifted it to glare at him defiantly. Blood from her lip ran down her chin.

"Put your weapons down. You're surrounded." The voice came from outside.

Diana scraped her foot along the shin of the guy still holding her, then stomped on his foot for good measure. He yelped and loosened his hold. An elbow to his face and Diana broke free. She lashed out again, knocking Kloch off balance as he half-turned toward the sound of the voice outside. She followed up with a punch to his face. His head snapped back, and he fell.

"Get down, Your Highness!" she shouted.

Kloch's men started firing through the windows into the street. A gun battle began. Diana pushed the sheikh, his son, and his daughter to the floor and then led them along the wall to the restaurant kitchen. They ran between the counters to a walk-in freezer at the back. Diana grabbed the door handle, opened the freezer, and pushed the three inside.

Back in the restaurant, the gunfire stopped. Diana peered into the dining area. Kloch's men were dead, their bodies strewn about. She registered a movement behind her, but instantly, a hand was put over her mouth, and she felt the muzzle of a gun at her temple. She could see Peter and his team inching forward outside.

"Your mother didn't suffer. It was very easy and calm. She did just what I told her like a little lamb." Kloch was breathing in Diana's ear. He pushed her through the swing door into the restaurant. "A tiny syringe in her arm was all it took. She fell asleep and never woke up. Your father, though? Now that was more violent."

Behind Kloch's hand, Diana was panting, her nostrils flaring, her eyes full of rage. There was a crash and the door to the restaurant flew open.

"Put the gun down, Hopkinson," Kloch ordered.

Peter looked at Diana. She gave him a small nod. Kloch had an arm at her chest, keeping her still, while the other held the gun to her head. Peter put his arms out in defeat. He slowly began to lower his gun to the floor. But then, Diana's knees gave way. She sagged, putting her weight on Kloch's arm, exposing his right flank.

Kloch's body twisted, unbalanced. "What the—"

Peter didn't hesitate. His gun was halfway to the ground but the bullet hit Kloch in the shoulder. It was a maneuver that required lightning reflexes and a crack

224 A. J. GOLDEN & GABRIELLA ZINNAS

shot. Peter made it look easy. He never even broke eye contact.

The blast knocked Kloch against the wall and he slid down to the bench. Diana ducked and ran. Panting and bloodied, Kloch sat loosely gripping his AK47, his other hand holding his injured shoulder. He winced with pain.

"Okay?" Peter asked Diana, still covering her. He wasn't taking any chances with Kloch.

"Yes, thank you," Diana mouthed. She sucked her lip. She didn't like being slapped. A noise behind them grabbed their attention.

"No! No!" Diana cried as she spun around.

Kloch slumped, his uninjured arm falling uselessly to his side. A black mark bloomed between his eyes, and blood trickled down his nose, a drip dropping to his chin. He stared, his eyes glassy, and his lips parted as he wilted and slid to the ground. His gun slipped from his hand, clattering onto the terracotta tiled floor.

"Damn, damn, dammit! I wanted him alive! I wanted him alive. He was the only person who knew, Peter, the only person who knew!"

Diana's fist thumped Peter's chest. He wound his arm around her neck and pulled her to him, kissing her hair and murmuring words she couldn't hear. Holding her, he waited until the worst of her despair had passed.

CHAPTER THIRTY-FIVE

PETER KICKED THE door closed with his foot. He was carrying two plastic bags of the best Indian food Vancouver could offer at this time of the morning. Why they'd needed to buy so much, he wasn't sure, but Diana insisted, and it didn't seem like the time to object.

Max came running, his claws clicking on the hardwood floor. Diana bent over to pick him up, but barely broke her stride, giving him only the quickest of squeezes, before placing him gently on the floor again.

Peter dropped the bag on the kitchen counter as Diana put plates in the oven to warm and rooted in drawers looking for a corkscrew. After the revelations of the day and the prospect of more to come, the content of the green bottle now standing next to the takeout was looking increasingly inviting.

Diana was silent, her face unreadable as she bustled around gathering silverware, plates, and napkins. Eating takeout this way was a new concept to Peter, but he appreciated the gesture, especially the cutlery. He had eaten curry with his fingers many times in the field alongside locals but never found it a very satisfactory experience. Cutlery enhanced many a dining experience in his opinion.

Peter looked at Diana thoughtfully as he held out a glass of red wine. She ignored him, deep in thought, until he tapped her on the shoulder with the back of his fingers. "Hey," he said softly, proffering the glass.

Diana looked down in surprise. Her shoulders dropped, and she let out the long breath she'd been holding in "Thanks." She took a swig without waiting for him.

"Are you alright?"

"I'm thinking."

"I can tell."

"So much to take in."

"Uh-huh." The silence descended once more.

Peter looked down at his feet, his wine glass cradled to his chest. It was 2 a.m. It had already been one hell of a day, even by his extensive standards. What kind of night was it going to be?

Diana pulled the plates from the oven, and they dished out the curry. The tops of the silver-lined white boxes were peeled back to reveal green, gold, red, and yellow dishes that always struck Peter as sights of beauty and not just because he loved the taste. He was starving, but as they settled down, not two bites into his meal, he decided to risk it.

"So . . ."

"Yes?"

"What *are* you thinking?"

"About what?"

"About everything. Your parents, Hawthorne, this so-called," Peter waved his fork around, "*cabal.*"

"You heard all that?"

"We flew a tiny drone through a window at the back of the restaurant. I heard it all."

"The Hawthorne thing is ridiculous, obviously. It can't possibly be true. My father was my father. They couldn't have hidden such an important detail from me for so long."

"Perhaps he didn't know. The timing . . ."

Diana's eyes hardened, but Peter didn't retreat. He held her gaze and counted. On the count of two, tears welled in Diana's eyes, and she trembled. He reached over and put his hand on hers.

"Could it be true?" Peter's eyes tried to meet hers, but Diana avoided his gaze. Instead, she lowered her head and stared at her plate, her lips pressed hard together as a tear rolled down her cheek. She gave the slightest of nods and then a deep, shuddering breath.

"My mom took my dad's name, but they never married. I don't know when they met exactly. I never thought about it. I certainly didn't ask."

"Do you know who this Neil Hawthorne is?"

Diana squeezed her eyes tight and shook her head. She turned her hand in Peter's and clutched it, her knuckles whitening. After a moment, she raised her head and took her hand away, wiping her eyes. She looked at him directly, her chin high.

"Come, there's something I want to show you." Diana stood and held her hand out. Obediently, Peter took it. He knew where she was taking him.

Diana led Peter along the hallway to the guest room, the door she always kept closed. Her heart was beating loudly in her chest. Her head twitched. Her mind was clear, however. She had never shown this room to anyone.

Diana opened the door to reveal a room almost bare of furniture, save for a white couch placed in the middle and a desk against one wall. Horizontal white blinds lay across the window. They were shuttered. The slightly off-white carpet beneath their feet was deep and luxurious. White closet doors filled most of the wall on the left side of the room. The walls were painted white.

Peter immediately saw that the blank décor served a purpose. It allowed the energy of the room to be taken up by something else. And that something else was powerful, pervasive, and bespoke of the passion that was Diana's alone.

All the walls were covered with items from her former life. The one she had when her parents were alive. There were photos of the three of them hung all around the room. One of her father holding Diana as a newborn, him looking down at her as she gazed back into his eyes. Another had Diana as a preschooler, her mother and father standing behind her with big smiles, their little girl squinting in the sun, a small frown creasing the bridge of her nose. Yet another had her standing in the Rose Garden at the University of British Columbia. Move-in day, probably. Once again, she was flanked by her parents, but this time her grin was broad while theirs looked wobbly, like they were stifling tears. But it was the rest of what was on the walls that intrigued Peter the most.

There was a whiteboard. Black lines connected the words that were written on it in blue. There were the names of Diana's parents and Liam Gregson, her father's partner, alongside dates, locations, and notes marked with an asterisk. In the corner, "Teddy" was followed by a question mark.

Peter swiveled his head, taking in the room, assessing. There were newspaper cuttings of the deaths covering the walls. Many were yellowing, but still clear and intact. Some,

Diana had laminated to protect them from light exposure and degradation over time. Neon sticky notes written in Diana's large, loopy hand punctuated the room with occasional spurts of color.

Diana hadn't let go of Peter's hand. She led him to the sofa. They sat in silence, looking straight ahead.

Finally, Diana broke the tension. "This is my parent's room."

"I guessed."

"This is where I come when I need to . . . need to, um, reflect."

Her hesitancy and the reality of her life struck Peter anew. This was her vulnerable spot. All the badassery and game-playing defensiveness stopped here. Here she was simply a woman making her way in the world the best she could under the most difficult of circumstances, without any support. He put his arm around her shoulders and drew her in. She lay her head on his shoulder.

"These are your parents, right?" He indicated a picture of the three of them.

"Yes, did you know about them?"

"Of course." He said it gently and smiled as he looked down at her. "You think I'd tackle suicide bombers with someone I didn't know? I ran a background check on you the first time I met you."

"Yes, yes, of course." Strangely, Diana felt bereft. All this time, her parent's death had felt like a private thing, a part of her that was held inside, closeted away from prying eyes. And here, Peter was telling her he'd known all along. It felt like a violation even though a small voice was telling her that checking her out was the sanest, safest route for Peter to take. "Why did you never say anything?"

"Because you never breathed a word about it. I may not

be the most sensitive person in the world, but I do realize that when someone doesn't say a single thing about something in their past of this magnitude, they don't want to talk about it. I figured I'd wait until you were ready."

"This is my control room. It's where I come when I need mental strength and clarity. It reminds me of who I am, and why I do what I do. I come in here to honor my parents' memory. And to work out who killed them.

Peter looked down at the floor. "I get it, I do. I have something I don't talk about too. Probably for the same reasons you don't."

"Oh?"

CHAPTER THIRTY-SIX

"I HAD A brother. Matthew. He was murdered three years ago. I have been doing the same thing for him that you have for your parents. Chasing people I need to hunt down.

"And have you succeeded?"

"No, the trail went cold immediately. I've made achingly slow progress, but I'm still determined, Diana. I will get them. They executed him in cold blood. He didn't deserve that."

"None of them do." Diana lifted her head and swiveled to look at him. "But there's more, isn't there?" Peter pursed his lips and stared straight ahead. "That kill shot today. No one does that, not from that distance. Not even Victoria Cross recipients with the rank of major."

"Not true. We're good at distance kill shots, we Canadians. Today's was comparatively short, a mere hop, skip, and a jump." They fell back into silence.

"So, are you going to tell me?" Diana asked, eventually. Peter didn't say anything. She was about to prompt him again.

"Black ops," he said quietly.

"How black?"

"Very. Jihadis mostly."

"Alone?"

"Usually, sometimes with a team."

"How long?"

"About fifteen months."

"How many?"

"One a month, roughly."

"That's a lot."

"After a few, it's just a job."

"Dead or alive?"

"Mostly dead, but sometimes we lifted the targets and passed them on when they were resourced for intel."

"They probably got passed to my people. Our worlds practically touched."

"Probably."

"Well, we're a pair, aren't we?"

"Uh-huh." They sat in silence for a few more moments.

"Why did you stop?"

"I'd had enough. I'd turned into a person I didn't recognize. I didn't feel anything anymore. The targets were just that, targets. Names on a list. Missions to be checked off, survived. When my brother died, I came to my senses. Matt was a father and a husband. He had people who loved him, who were dependent on him. They suffered more from his death than he did. The people I killed had children, wives, parents, too. A chink appeared in my armor, and my perspective changed. From then on, it was either I got out, or I got killed. I believed in the work, but I'd lost the edge I needed to do it. I had to get out. And I had things I needed to do here at home."

"Did TFI come for you? You're a perfect match for them."

"Lennox offered me a position that would have meant more strategy, less fieldwork. I wanted to take it, but my head wasn't in the right place for any of it."

"So how off-book were you?"

"Complete, total, and utter. I lived in the field and went wherever I was needed. For those fifteen months, I didn't exist. I roamed the world alone, never contacting anyone, just floating and responding to orders."

"So all that guff in Dubai about never being compromised was just that. Guff?"

"No, I'm okay with what I did. I am on the side of right and good. And I know what is right and good. These were bad, bad people I was dispatching. I had the stomach to do what was necessary, and I did ugly work for the greater good. And I worked with the bravest, most honest people I will ever meet, some of whom laid down their lives for me. But I have no interest in doing it now. My time for that is over. I meant what I said earlier. We're in danger of losing ourselves when we're at war. But I found my way back. You did, too. We're lucky. Some people never do."

"But how can I trust you? I had you vetted so I could tell you all my secrets, and you argued with me for keeping things from you. And yet here you are, the biggest keeper of secrets of all!"

Peter flushed. "Yes, you're right, and I'm sorry. I've been unfair and jealous and unreasonable. I apologize. You know how dark this is, and I thought you might be compromised if I told you." He sighed. "But mostly, I was scared about how you'd react. Getting the girl when you do what I did only happens in movies. I'm hoping that we've saved each other's asses enough times to get beyond this."

"You realize that being with me puts you in danger from this . . . this . . . whatever this is?" Diana waved at the cuttings and photos on the wall.

"Tell me something I don't know. You've been a serious danger to my health from the beginning, lady. Heart attacks, high blood pressure . . . Peter trailed off. "Broken heart," he added quietly.

"I haven't broken your heart, have I?"

"You've put me through the wringer a few times."

"I'm sorry." Diana looked down at her lap. "Is this all? I mean, is there anything else?"

"No, this is it. Promise. There's nothing more. You?"

"No."

Silently, they stared straight ahead, processing everything that had happened that day. Something inside Diana shifted. It felt like an earthquake had moved the ground on which she walked. A seismic shift had taken place. Nothing was the same. Nothing. The prism through which she viewed the world had changed. The people she thought she knew so well were different. And yet she felt stronger, more determined, more focused, more *alive,* than ever.

She let her eyes fall on her favorite photo of her parents. Her eyes softened. She lay her head back down on Peter's shoulder. He didn't move except to give her arm a gentle squeeze.

"So, first thing tomorrow?" he said.

"Hmm?

"Neil Hawthorne."

"Yes. First thing." Diana closed her eyes. "Thank you."

Max watched them from the doorway. All he could see were the tops of their heads peeking over the back of the sofa. He stayed where he was in the hallway, keeping his front paws neatly together, knowing somehow not to disturb them. When his humans didn't move, Max settled down, crossing his paws in front of him. He had all the time in the world. All he had to do was wait.

Thank you for reading *Exposed*! I hope you love Diana as much as I do. If you would like to receive the exclusive prequel to the Diana Hunter series and learn more about Diana's parents, their murders and her backstory, what drives her so, as well as find out about new books

and receive great bonuses, please sign up for my newsletter: https://www.alisongolden.com.

In the next book in the series, *Broken*, the situation gets tense for Diana. When twenty-two young women are abandoned on a train track, Diana is thrust into a labyrinth of deception and danger. Every step draws Diana deeper into a plot that challenges her every belief about justice and morality. She must decide who to trust, who to save, and who to bring to justice. Loyalty and treachery collide. With the clock ticking, Diana faces an impossible choice: save those she loves or sacrifice everything for the greater good? Get your copy of Broken from Amazon now! Broken is FREE in Kindle Unlimited.

If you love the Diana Hunter series, you'll also love the Roxy Reinhardt mysteries. Will Roxy triumph after her life falls apart? She's fired from her job, her boyfriend dumps her, she's out of money. So, on a whim, she goes on the trip of a lifetime to New Orleans. There, she gets mixed up in a Mardi Gras murder. *Things were going to be fine. They were, weren't they?* Get the first in the series, Mardi Gras Madness from Amazon. Also FREE in Kindle Unlimited.

If you're looking for a detective series with twisty plots and characters that feel like friends, binge read the *USA Today* bestselling Inspector Graham series featuring a new and unusual detective with a phenomenal memory and a tragic past. The first in the series, *The Case of the Screaming Beauty* is available for purchase from Amazon and FREE in Kindle Unlimited.

And don't miss the sweet, funny *USA Today* bestselling Reverend Annabelle Dixon series featuring a madcap, lovable lady vicar whose passion for cake is matched only by her desire for justice. The first in the series, *Death at the Café* is available for purchase from Amazon. Like all my books, *Death at the Café* is FREE in Kindle Unlimited.

I hugely appreciate your help in spreading the word about *Exposed*, including telling a friend. Reviews help readers find books! Please leave a review on your favorite book site.

Turn the page for an excerpt from the first book in the Roxy Reinhardt mystery series, *Mardi Gras Madness* . . .

USA TODAY BESTSELLING AUTHOR

A.J.GOLDEN

GABRIELLA ZINNAS

BROKEN

A DIANA HUNTER MYSTERY

BROKEN
CHAPTER ONE

"UNCLE PEEP!" DIANA got out of the car and turned to see a young girl run up to Peter. She was aged about seven, in a pink dress with white flowers and green rain boots. The girl wrapped her arms around Peter's thighs and looked up at him adoringly, wrinkling her nose and beaming to reveal two perfect rows of white milk teeth and gums so pink they matched her dress.

Peter's face lit up. "Hey, kiddo!" In one clean motion, Peter bent and swung the girl round onto his back, where she clung, her cheek pressed between his shoulder blades.

"Leth go!" the girl lisped. The thick lenses of her blue-rimmed glasses reflected the sunshine but didn't disguise the almond shape and upward slant of her eyes.

Peter marched into the garden and placed the girl at the top of the plastic slide that sat in the middle before running around to the bottom to catch her as she slid down. It was clearly an established ritual, because as soon as Peter caught her, he swung her up to the top of the slide, and down she slid again. Diana watched from outside the unpainted picket fence that surrounded the backyard.

The yard had an uncared-for air about it. Weed grasses grew tall under the slide, while dead, brown grass interspersed with stretches of dirt covered the rest of it. Old, untended shrubs grew wild and rambling around the edges, the flowers small, the leaves pale and sparse, holding on despite a lack of attention. But uncle and niece were oblivious to their surroundings as they horsed around, throwing themselves, quite literally, into their play.

"He didn't tell you about Clare's Down syndrome?" Diana turned, a little embarrassed that she'd been caught staring. A woman a few years older than she walked toward Diana, her arms folded. She looked cold, or defensive.

"No, he didn't."

"Well, he's told us a lot about you." The woman looked at Diana carefully. The end of her nose was red, her cheeks too, while her curly, fair hair created a messy halo around her head. She wore a grey, crew neck Fair Isle sweater patched at the elbows and faded jeans. Diana instinctively understood she was being scrutinized.

The woman held out her hand. "I'm Shannon, Peter's sister-in-law. But you probably already knew that."

Diana smiled. "Diana."

She nodded over to where Peter was now galloping around the yard with Clare on his back, Clare squealing with delight as she bounced along. Peter stopped abruptly, lifted Clare over his head, and held her upside down by her ankles, giving her a gentle shake before dropping her carefully to the ground.

"Do they always do that?" Diana said. Mirroring Shannon, she folded her arms. This was a side of Peter Diana hadn't seen. He seemed to be enjoying himself. She hoped she wouldn't be encouraged to join in. Diana looked down at her shoes. She hadn't come dressed for play.

"Always. At least they're outside. It's a bit much when they do it in the living room." Shannon chuckled, then sobered. "It's great for Clare to have this kind of rough and tumble play, though. She doesn't get it otherwise, and you can see she hates it." Clare was now rolling in the dirt, giggling as Peter tickled her.

"I thought they sang in the living room. Peter's the cameraman, he told me. Clare sings songs from *Frozen*."

"Yeah, they do. That's a whole other thing. Then there's the cheer she leads him in. He follows the moves faithfully, while she orders him around and gives him a talking-to when he gets it wrong. It's quite comical, really. Peter's a great guy. I don't know what we'd do without him." Shannon looked at Diana as she chewed her lip, her gaze lingering as Diana's big grey eyes held hers. Diana blinked first, and the two women turned to watch uncle and niece in silence for a few seconds before Shannon spoke again. "Come on inside. I'll make you some coffee."

A small gesture of welcome. It wasn't much, but it was something. "That would be lovely, thank you," Diana replied.

Inside, Shannon busied herself making Diana's coffee. The scruffy kitchen smelled of boiled vegetables. A pan of beans in an orange sauce sat on the worktop. "Sorry, it's instant."

"Hey, don't be. I love it. Reminds me of when I was a kid. My mom used to make me a milky instant coffee every morning. These days, of course, they've turned making them into a performance art, and we go around calling them silly names like lattes, but at their heart, they're the same thing. Milky coffee." Diana took a sip of her drink as she cringed inwardly, unsure if she had been patronizing. She closed her eyes. "Hmm, delish. Thank you."

"Let's sit down. The other two probably won't notice we're even here. Peter said you were on your way to something or other."

"Yeah, nothing very interesting. We've been invited to a demo of a new piece of software the city is rolling out. It's supposed to help us catch a few more bad guys. We'll see." Diana took another sip of her coffee. "How long have you lived here?"

"Just a couple of years. When Matt, my husband . . . Peter's brother . . . died, we moved to this." Shannon pulled a face. "It's not what we're used to, but it's all I could afford. I need to be home for Clare, to give her stability, take her to appointments . . ." Shannon trailed off before rallying. She took a deep breath and slapped her thighs. "Peter helps us out. He's been an absolute rock." She gave a tight smile. "Peter said your parents were murdered too."

"Yes." Phew, that got heavy quickly. "Over a decade ago now."

"I'm sorry. That must have been hard."

Diana nodded, racking her brain for a safer subject to segue onto, but for some reason she couldn't come up with one. "I've survived." She smiled. "And I have my little dog, Max."

Shannon returned Diana's smile. "Ah, we've heard a lot about Max. Clare's dying to meet him."

"We'll have to arrange it!" Diana said, happy to be on safer conversational ground. Max got her out of a lot of holes.

The sounds of banging and chatter reached them. A moment later, Clare came rushing in. She put her hands on Shannon's thighs and looked appealingly at her mother, her eyes wide and innocent behind her glasses. "Uncle Peep says he has to go. Make him stay, Mommy! Make him stay!"

Shannon swept Clare's bangs from her face and looked deep into her eyes. "Remember I told you, it's just a short visit today. Do you want to say hello to his friend Diana?" Immediately, Clare spun around to notice Diana for the first time. If Shannon had thought her entreaty would be met positively, she was wrong. Clare's eyes flashed dangerously as she regarded "Peter's friend." Diana smiled and opened her mouth to say "hi," but Clare got in first.

"No!" Diana started at the sound, surprised. Clare immediately ran from the room, leaving the two women in an embarrassed silence.

"Oh, dear," Diana said.

"She'll recover. Clare's used to having Peter to herself. I didn't think she'd be quite that sensitive, though. Sorry. I'll go and talk to her."

"She's smarter than we give her credit for." Peter appeared in the doorway, panting slightly, his breath disturbing the strands of hair that fell across his forehead, his cheeks glowing. "I'm sorry we can't stay longer to bring her around. We have to get going."

"Yeah, okay, let me just get her though so you don't leave with her like this."

"I'll go," Peter said. He disappeared up the stairs.

Shannon smiled awkwardly at Diana. Diana gave her a tight smile back. The idea crossed Diana's mind that perhaps she should have thought this visit through more carefully. Peter had suggested they drop in on their way to the Vancouver Convention Center. Shannon lived just a few minutes away. It had seemed innocent enough—a quick visit to "break the ice" with the two people who mattered most to Peter. Now they were faced with the longer-term ramifications of a threatened little girl who thought Diana would usurp her in her beloved uncle's affections.

Peter returned with Clare, her head buried in his neck. She carried a soft, plush, pink pony. "See? We're all friends."

"But you're leaving," Clare moaned, her voice muffled as she mumbled into his neck.

"I'll be back soon."

Clare lifted her head and glared at Diana. "Not with her."

"Clare . . ." Shannon warned her.

"No!" Clare turned her face into Peter's neck again. Peter rolled his eyes and half-turned from the two women, murmuring in Clare's ear. Diana noticed him pull his watch off his wrist and offer it to his niece, who nodded sulkily and took it from him. He turned back to the women, kissed Clare's head, and handed her to Shannon.

"Say buh-bye, Clare," Shannon said. The little girl muttered. "What was that?

"Bye," Clare whispered.

"Bye, Clare. Nice to meet you," Diana said brightly. She could not wait to leave.

"I'll drop by tomorrow, Shannon," Peter said. "For a bit longer." He kissed her on the cheek and left through the back door.

Diana made to follow him, but as she walked by, Shannon stopped her, placing a hand on her arm. Diana looked down at Shannon's hand and then into her eyes, seeing a fiery determination in them. "Peter's a great guy. He's been like a father to Clare. He put his glittering career on hold to come back and support us after Matt died. We're very protective of him. I've never seen him care about a girl like he does you. Don't mess him around, okay?"

To get your copy of Broken visit the link below:
https://www.alisongolden.com/broken

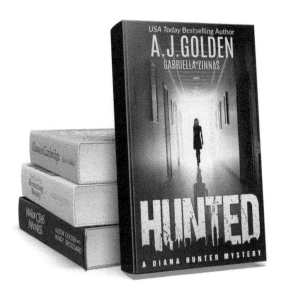

"Your emails seem to come on days when I need to read them because they are so upbeat."
- Linda W -

For a limited time, you can get the first books in each of my series - *Chaos in Cambridge, Hunted* (exclusively for subscribers - not available anywhere else), *The Case of the Screaming Beauty, and Mardi Gras Madness* - plus updates about new releases, promotions, and other Insider exclusives, by signing up for my mailing list at:

https://www.alisongolden.com/diana

TAKE MY QUIZ

What kind of mystery reader are you? Take my thirty second quiz to find out!

https://www.alisongolden.com/quiz

BOOKS IN THE DIANA HUNTER SERIES

Hunted (Prequel)

Snatched

Stolen

Chopped

Exposed

Broken

COLLECTIONS

Books 1-3

Snatched

Stolen

Chopped

ALSO BY A. J. GOLDEN

Fireworks in France

Witches at the Wedding

FEATURING ROXY REINHARDT

Mardi Gras Madness

New Orleans Nightmare

Louisiana Lies

Cajun Catastrophe

ABOUT THE AUTHOR

Alison Golden is the *USA Today* bestselling author of the Inspector David Graham mysteries, a traditional British detective series, and two cozy mystery series featuring main characters Reverend Annabelle Dixon and Roxy Reinhardt. As A. J. Golden, she writes the Diana Hunter thriller series.

Alison was raised in Bedfordshire, England. Her aim is to write stories that are designed to entertain, amuse, and calm. Her approach is to combine creative ideas with excellent writing and edit, edit, edit. Alison's mission is simple: To write excellent books that have readers clamouring for more.

Alison is based in the San Francisco Bay Area with her husband and twin sons. She splits her time between London and San Francisco.

For up-to-date promotions and release dates of upcoming books, sign up for the latest news here: https://www. alisongolden.com/diana.

For more information:
www.alisongolden.com
alison@alisongolden.com

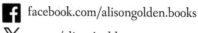 facebook.com/alisongolden.books

X x.com/alisonjgolden

instagram.com/alisonjgolden

THANK YOU

Thank you for taking the time to read *Exposed*. If you enjoyed it, please consider telling your friends or posting a short review. Word of mouth is an author's best friend and very much appreciated.

Thank you,

Printed in the USA
CPSIA information can be obtained
at www.ICGtesting.com
LVHW092312140824
788309LV00030B/415